Cerberus & Cigarette's

re·sil·ience

the capacity to recover quickly from difficulties; toughness.

(Google)

Prelude

Cerberus limped as quickly as his three legs allowed him to limp. His tail was tucked tight under his abdomen as if it were frightened of being left behind, and his ears duplicated this tension as they pressed firmly against his head. There was a dull ache building on one side of his chest, and on the other side there remained a collage of various liquids and bits of food where his body struck the ground. Fear quelled any urge he had to nurse his wounds or clean himself. Little yellow droplets of his own urine indirectly linked the room he had fled with the storage room where he now lay. His closet cave provided a thin sense of security, since its position amplified the intensity of the screams and commotion coming from the kitchen.

"My God! Stop, Norton!" someone screamed.

Cerberus flinched.

"You're going to slice yourself to pieces. Please give me your hand!" the same voice went on demanding.

The words meant nothing to the dog. The anger in the voices had him tuck his head deeper under his paw as if this would help to dull every detail jolting his incredible sense of hearing.

He felt like a coward for running away but was glued to the ground, shivering uncontrollably. Pain and shame took turns washing over him. His masters and his friends appeared to be in trouble, but why? Cerberus had sensed something serious was wrong, as there usually was when people were gathered close together yelling at one another. When he had approached the noise, he'd been confronted by the thick, acrid smell of fear. Now his own fear was worse than that of getting kicked or even of losing a limb. His greatest fear was that he would lose those he loved and be left alone once again.

Chapter 1, Daily News

Aadir Manji spent most of his free time inside the contrived settings of the various coffee shops that were a long walk or a short bus ride from the house he had lived in his entire life. His beaming pregnant mother and thrilled father had rented the small but well-lit second floor of a triplex a month before he was born, and it had grown smaller around him each day thereafter. The home was complete with one bedroom, one bathroom, and one room that comprised dining room, kitchen, and living room. Originally there was also a storage room that served as a utility closet and which kept the washing machine and dryer. It was small, and the family was happy there.

By the time Aadir began walking confidently upright, he was already speaking his mind. He let his parents know that the fact that he still slept in a crib was appalling to him, and he enjoyed repeating "A man needs his own space!" He must have heard that somewhere on television and he repeated, "A man needs his own space!" throughout the day, for weeks, while his parents tried to convince him to be patient. They even removed the rails from Aadir's crib, but this proved insufficient. To quell his nagging, his parents took the washing machine and dryer out of the old storage room and placed them in what became a cramped entryway. They put a single bed in the makeshift bedroom and did their best to cover up the electrical panels and exposed plumbing with magazine pictures of motorbikes and a few posters of animals and landscapes they felt would make the space more kid-friendly.

Once Aadir's new kingdom was complete, Aadir was terrified to actually stay in it. To his credit, he never mentioned this to his father. He did once cry to his mom about the scary sounds and bad dreams he had in the old storage room. His mother talked convincingly through his tears and assured him that being "a man" required following through with things and confronting one's fears directly. After smearing an impressive amount of snot and tears on his sleeve, he then jumped off his mother's lap, marched back into his tiny room, and yelled, "Get lost, everything that isn't me! I am king here and this is my room, in my house! So get out!"

He pictured the imaginary beasts and ghosts squeezing out of the corners of the tiny room, running in fear of their new emperor. His mother took him to the local big-box store and helped him redecorate a bit on a tight budget. At this point he took ownership of the space, and he never complained again. About almost anything.

It was indicative of puberty that Aadir began wanting nothing to do with the very space he had desired so strongly before. He frequented local cafés constantly. This was less an attempt to escape the suffocating space than to escape his usually despondent and sullen father. When Aadir was fifteen, his mother died suddenly of a massive stroke. There were no warning signs, and there was no saving her. She slumped over one weekday night at dinner right after asking Aadir, "How do you like this fresh bread I bought? I got it … I got it, I …."

That was it. Well, that wasn't entirely it. There were the few seconds of convulsions, and there were nearly twenty minutes of him and his dad taking turns giving her CPR. When the ambulance arrived, the remainder of the three-person family initially felt relief, imagining that she might be okay in the hands of professionals. Unfortunately, she was clearly gone. The paramedics assured the boy and his father that they had already done everything they could have done prior to getting help and commended them for such brave work. Then they took Aadir's mother away.

Aadir's father, Sonny, had done his best to keep a strong and pleasant attitude for his son, especially during the two years before Aadir's high school graduation. It was clear that he was avoiding the reality that his wife was not coming back, and he never went to see any friends or family after the funeral service. Eventually those who had once cared so much about him stopped coming around to cheer him up. Sonny often buried himself in extra overtime hours and weekend odd jobs to keep money coming in after his wife was gone. The rest of the time he spent purposefully with Aadir. He cooked him his meals, he reviewed his homework, he drove him to participate in sports and to practices, and he even took his son on short hikes and to cafés on Sundays. All these distractions began to wear thin, however, and by the time Aadir had gotten his diploma, Sonny resembled very little of the great man he'd once been.

Being around Sonny too much at this point was poisonous. *It was the government's fault. It was the system's fault. It was the farmer's and food companies' fault...* It was every corporation in the world's fault that his wife had died, and the world in every way was a hopeless and worthless place to live. To Sonny, the human condition grew worse each day, as every basic freedom was constricted. To Sonny, each day was another benchmark, dooming the soul of every person or parasite to a deeper, more painful place in the salivating mouth of hell. Nothing was as good as it used to be, and nothing would ever be as good as it once was.

Aadir would sometimes still challenge his father's ramblings, even when they were fairly accurate, but Sonny would say that he had already made his mind up.

"You have so much to learn my boy," Sonny would passively repeat when challenged.

For some reason, his father insisted that his new cynical worldview had nothing to do with the loss of Aadir's mother, and that it was solely due to the reality of conditions on earth at that given moment.

"Unfortunately, Aadir, it is only logical that conditions will grow worse for every living thing on earth until the end of times."

As horribly depressing as these conversations were, at least Aadir saw a spark in his father on such occasions. Otherwise, Sonny seemed to feel it was entirely his fault that his wife was gone, and he was here to live in purgatory without her. It was when Sonny dug himself into a self-deprecating depression that he became truly intolerable. So Aadir would go grab some coffee and hang out at a shop for several hours. Aadir had decided that living with the guilt of all these temporary abandonments was healthier than being sucked into tandem hopelessness.

Nothing Aadir attempted seemed to help and eventually depression began consuming his father. Whenever he wasn't working, Sonny would spend his time crying in bed. Then he began to cry at the table and on the couch at mealtimes. Eventually he began to lose weight and forget to cook, eat, bathe, and show up to work. Because of this, his job was terminated shortly before his scheduled retirement. Unexpectedly, the tech company to which Sonny had been so dedicated actually continued to compensate him. It seemed like his previous charm and enthusiastic dedication had not been forgotten by someone of influence. It was at this point that Sonny had given Aadir his passwords for his online banking and credit cards, along with access to all of his personal information. Then Sonny stopped leaving the house and finally stopped speaking. Aadir estimated that there would be enough money for his father to survive at home for the rest of his life as long as the finances were managed carefully.

Aadir felt the strongest sense of duty to his father and made up his mind to stay with him. The only other option would have been contacting social services, but after doing some research he determined that the end result of such an action would land Sonny in a position where he would require a full-time caretaker. This was not what his father desired and would not suffice, so Aadir chose to become the caretaker. He now had to prepare all Sonny's meals, buy the groceries, do the laundry, clean the house, and ensure that, to the outside world, things were copacetic in their home. He prayed that if all the bills were paid and the house was kept up, no one would come looking for problems. He could even convince his father to go out on occasional walks with him on days that were good both weather-wise and Sonny-wise. Being seen around the neighborhood might have seemed like progress, but very little changed.

After his father's mental deterioration, Aadir stopped living like a spoiled prospective prodigy. He traded in his flashy athletic gear and the shoes he had for every occasion for a simple—albeit fashionable—wardrobe. He did his best to find a balance between durable clothes that still complemented his style and stature. Price, however, was always the issue of contention, and he even bartered with the various thrift shops he frequented. Aadir refused to spend any of his father's money for things outside the home and these decisions cost him a few relationships. He quickly shed friends who were convinced that spending was living. Even though taking care of Sonny was a full-time job, Aadir would use Sonny's bank account only to take care of his father, to bring food and supplies into the home, and to keep the IRS and utility companies at bay.

Aadir would have felt irreparable guilt for spending any of the money his father had worked so hard for and sacrificed so much for, while he still lived under his roof. His food and a warm place to sleep had always been covered entirely by his father's funds, and he greatly appreciated this. On the other hand, part of Aadir's frugality was associated with his fear of the unexpected. He couldn't help but buy into some of what his father and what the news repeated: *The human condition was changing too rapidly to safely regulate, mistakes will be soon be made that will spell humanities doom.* He felt turmoil mounting and figured that he and his nearly incapacitated father could be forced from their residence at any time. Each month, after Sonny's check from the tech company was cashed, Aadir would stash the money in steel containers that he had put in place behind refinished drywall. The stacked cash provided fairly adequate replacement insulation.

Since Aadir used only the small amounts of cash he got from late night odd jobs, he ended up spending a lot of time in inexpensive places. One of these places ended up being the nearby restaurant, Cigarette's. As his days became more routine and comfortable, time began to slip away.

***

Aadir looked at the clock on his table screen. It was after noon. All morning he had been managing dozens of pages of electronic information simultaneously and effectively, which was a fairly complex feat. Aadir wrote opinion columns for several different websites, some of which paid him. Often he would never physically see the product, place, or even meet the person he was blogging about. He was, however, a very accomplished researcher, constantly highlighting, chronicling, and filtering information. This competency gained him a great deal of respect in many online communities. His handle was @aadirwins on all social media but few people knew his actual identity.

He could hear the waiter walking up behind him.

"Can I get another latte, please, Steven?" he asked. Steven had actually let Aadir in at seven thirty that morning, half an hour before Cigarette's was meant to open.

"That'll be two coffees and a sandwich today! We are going to grow rich off you yet!" Steven replied.

"I tend to require less than most people, so if I end up having anything else, I may think this place is turning me into a glutton."

"Then my mission will be complete," Steven said happily. "I'll be right back with a first class latte."

Aadir had always been a thin man. Every major movement he made enabled the onlooker to see the entire mechanics of the muscles and ligaments it took to operate his body. Lean muscles, primarily developed from yoga, covered his skeletal frame.

Steven returned a few minutes later with a frothy brimming cup that had a cartoon castle on the side.

"Thank you," Aadir said, taking a sip.

"You're welcome my friend. So who was that pretty girl you were chatting it up with this morning? I've seen her here alone but never in your charming company before."

"Her name is Anna."

"A girlfriend?"

"Hopefully *the* girlfriend," Aadir replied. "Super smart, caring, good sense of humor ..."

Steven took this opportunity to conduct his own evaluation of the newcomer. "She better like our food."

"Oh, she'll love it. In fact we are planning on having dinner here tomorrow. Any idea what the special might be?"

"Burgers, my friend. But not just any burgers, these are not to be missed. We tried out a new recipe last night, and if we get good feedback we will be adding them to our *preferred* customers menu permanently."

"I seriously can't wait. You guys never disappoint." Aadir said.

"True, but you and your new beau better like it hot," Steven said, attaching a spicy attitude to his words.

Aadir laughed. "Well, we will certainly be finding out soon enough. I am really hoping this goes well; I haven't been this excited in a long time."

For a self-ascertained righteous geek, Aadir was also brilliantly social. He was never one to feel like he had to hide the information he was digesting. He delighted in sharing his knowledge, and he delighted in listening and digging further. When someone sat down, the table screen would automatically divide equally between each person, so everyone had an automatic workstation. If anyone chose to disagree with Aadir on something he was currently passionate about, he would begin browsing through several pages of information that would support his claim and undermine his opponent as they were talking. On slower days, Steven would occasionally sit down for a debate.

These conversations were usually about current events, and Aadir would barely break eye contact as the two volleyed questions across the table. By the time Aadir had found enough to formulate his argument and interject, Steven would already have a vague idea what was coming, as he would have seen flashes of pictured evidence countering his claims. Aadir would then electronically flip the screen around and present his case, while pointing to various forms of support for arguments that were upside down to him and right side up to Steven. His methods were magical and frustratingly belittling.

The whole time, he would be impulsively shaking his hands and feet to the point that Steven once asked him if he had a disorder.

"No, no, I'm still in pretty good order," Aadir replied. "All my energy has to go somewhere, and I guess my body just likes to shake it out?"

His actions always reflected earnestness and caring, but it was just that no one seemed as smart to Aadir as Aadir did. This type of narcissism was earned from a lifetime of solving problems alone. His whole life was a mess of perceived progress in an artificial world and much less progress otherwise. His mastery of information and, to many, misinformation was proof of his earlier trials. He was blissfully ignorant of the fact that his comedy of facts was constantly changing.

Aadir broke from looking at his screen to watch Steven pick up a soiled napkin from the floor near his table. He must have inadvertently brushed it off while he was wailing away at the key pad.

"Oh, sorry about that Steven..."

"Not to worry, it's not the first time I've grabbed things from the floor as you spaz away at whatever it is you do here."

Aadir chuckled, "I don't doubt that."

"Are you going to be needing anything other than the coffee Aadir? I'm going to help Josef with a bit of cleaning before the rush starts."

"Nothing more for me, I'll try to catch you to pay up before I go."

It was Steven who caught a laugh this time, "Ha! For such an honor I'll certainly make myself available."

Chapter 2, Transitions

Every public bathroom looked like the alleyway behind a waterless, squalid shack inhabited by glue-sniffing evolutionary throwbacks, and every public school and general hospital was home to rats voiding themselves at will, like their drug-addicted brethren. The last three years had seen a televised campaign that encouraged people to clean up after themselves, while at the same time the custodians' union was being dismantled. The remaining janitors were dreadful, teary-eyed, aging beasts pitied by the unemployable.

Alternatively, every pizza, donair, sandwich, sushi and burger joint looked like a seamless laboratory housing mysterious scientists who were busy creating as good a product as they could from the standardized meats, flours, sauces, herbs, sweeteners, milk-like products, and produce they were forced to buy in order to remain open. People told stories of a time around a century earlier when public facilities were kept pristine while private businesses were often shabby and suspect. This concept now seemed wildly foreign and perhaps even un-American.

Legends still lived on, though, and real food could still be found. Secret spices and sauces were literally a secret and were added to bland meals for a small extra cost or were concealed by rebel chefs until they became encouraged enough by the loyalty of return clientele. Health inspectors' efforts to duplicate this behavior were constantly transparent, but occasionally a tired owner would have a bottle of his precious sauce seized and replaced by a healthy fine. With all their downsides, restaurants were still incredibly popular for entrepreneurs. The concept was simple: "everyone eats."

It was in one of these restaurants, a place named Cigarette's, that Aadir and Anna sat across from each other, as they had done dozens of times before. They were bent on getting a fix of good food that was now nearly as illegal as oven-baked drugs.

Anna's exotic, pale, makeup-free mouth chowed her burger vigorously behind svelte fingers. Atop her gangly frame her thin, symmetrical shoulders and collarbone shone brightly and naked, exposed above a cyclone of the deep purple and black materials surrounding most of her body. Her burger was so hot with its brine of prohibited peppers that tiny beads of sweat appeared on her upper lip. She quickly and repeatedly dabbed at them with her thick sleeve, continuously avoiding the same greasy sleeve-spot in order to reduce the risk of getting burger pimples.

She looked across at Aadir, who appeared supremely relaxed. He had his back against the window at the end of the hard, fake wood-grain booth in which he sat. His dark and slightly dirty sandaled feet hung out the other end of the food cubicle, endangering passersby. His face was the color of a heaping tablespoon of cocoa stirred into a liter of milk, and his ethnicity was a crapshoot. Wild, loosely curled hair stuck out underneath a ridiculously oversized faded-green beret that was clearly a treasured piece of individualism. Aadir's left foot shook to no discernible beat. Anna had watched his wriggling toes dangle from the various booths of their favorite restaurant for the past two years.

Anna knew that equating Aadir with relaxation was ridiculous. Although he was often smiling, was relaxed in spirit, and even made a valiant effort to listen when people spoke to him, he was always waiting to say something. He yearned to dig into ideas and conversation. When he spoke, his hands would divide the air, his fists would clench and pound the table, he would pull at his wild hair and play with his ridiculous hat. In silence he would sketch and scrape, hum, drum his fingers, and otherwise irritate Anna as she attempted to read or have a conversation with someone other than him for a moment.

After Aadir was finished orating his most recent of thoughts, Anna swallowed an under-chewed bite of meat hard, and after crushing a greasy napkin in her hand and whacking her chest gently with the outstretched thumb of her fist, she cleared her throat and challenged Aadir, as she so often did.

"So, you think that faith is just some slide rule that measures an individual's experience?"

"Yes," replied Aadir, unfazed and not overly indignantly. "You are basically a convenience-Christian. Your brown-skinned parents were for some reason Christians, and therefore you became a believer as well. You have to admit that it's surprising that through the confusion of childhood and the fact that you had many other friends of Middle Eastern descent, you somehow never really explored Hinduism, Islam, or Buddhism?"

Aadir's tone was even and kind, but nearly everything he had said was patronizing, sexist, and even racist. The two lovers shared a liberating—albeit strange—level of free-flowing thought.

Anna was slightly offended, but as usual she decided to ignore her feelings.

"I don't see how that is surprising," she said. "Most of my friends never even bothered to commit to the most basic of their forebears' traditions, regardless of their beliefs. I was brought up to believe that Jesus was a man of great influence who once lived, just like us, well … much harder than us, I suppose. But even under dire, distressing, and painful experiences he sacrificed himself to promote goodness, tolerance, and kindness and *empowered* people with faith and the pursuit of cooperation."

"I dig cooperation," Aadir said, staring back at Anna, obviously engaged by her words. His eyes were living projectors of happiness framed in large black glasses. His glasses cost more than the laser surgery that could have easily fixed his nearsightedness. Anna thought that this was ridiculous. She also thought that Aadir looked sexy in the spectacles and only let him know how foolish he was for having glasses since he mistreated them so often when he was distracted.

"Plus"—she paused to stuff a few seasoned fries into her mouth, not shy about talking while hiding the mush in her cheek— "the Bible is just like any other historical text. That might not be saying much, but many of the lessons and ideas remain true. In the end the idea is to unite people who may otherwise be convinced that the evil they see and the indifference they have experienced are the best reflection of actuality."

Aadir opened his palms in a somewhat dismissive fashion. "I just can't support a fantasy novel about a monotheistic idea that has led to more death than any other text in history."

Anna felt a little discouraged by Aadir's arrogance. She took a manageable bite of her burger and, with a small amount of food still processing in her mouth, she continued, holding her sandwich and shaking it as she spoke. A few droplets of greasy mustard and hot sauce missed the plate.

"Does that mean that you are too righteous to take joy in people gathering together, volunteering, providing support for each other? It isn't the Middle Ages anymore, A."

A, was Anna's pet name for Aadir that she usually chose to use when his behavior became tiresome. His behavior became tiresome several times a day. The life and passion he possessed far outweighed this inconvenience, however, and Anna knew this deeply and loved him unwaveringly. She gulped down the tasty remainder of her meal.

Anna could see that Aadir had barely touched his food and instead was perusing the Internet on the screen in front of him. He did not reference anything from his efforts, so he must not have found what he was looking for. He continued pushing the conversation in spite of this.

"Can't people just gather at community halls and help each other out there?" This was all he could pull up in an instant.

"*What* community halls, Aadir? Do you know where the nearest one is? No. You don't. I, on the other hand, volunteer at two such facilities that are currently full of special needs children in the morning, soup lines in the afternoon, and municipal action-slash-development meetings during the evenings and night. Not only can you not find the time to use these places if you wanted to, but what government faction would ever fund these doomed facilities if they were to be used for people's spiritual benefit? And they stink! Yes, they actually *smell*. Don't honest and good people deserve better than this when challenging their deepest questions, confronting their fears, and when searching for just a little bit of solace in all this day-to-day garbage we deal with?"

Aadir lowered his voice, reflecting his waning confidence in the argument. "I'd imagine there would be more funding for community places if they weren't so many different religions trying to divide everyone up."

Anna sighed. "This argument is draining and passé, Aadir. You have to come at me with a better lunchtime concept than this, or we may as well be discussing last week's weather."

"Don't I usually?" Aadir pried, mock-sheepishly.

"Yes, you do. But I would say more like 'occasionally' than 'usually' these days," Anna replied, with half a smile and squinty bright eyes. She reached over the table and grasped Aadir's hands.

Chapter 3, Clarity

Anna was born into a home that already contained third- and fourth-generation Indian Americans. There was only a hint of Eastern pronunciation in her grandparents' speech, and for the most part she felt indistinguishable from other girls in her town. Her nuclear family's home was situated on the outskirts of a tranquil and tolerably poor town in the hillsides of southeastern Oregon. What she remembered most was that it was an exceedingly wet place in which to grow up. Moisture came frequently, with a bounty of snow every winter and misty, lush, pulsating greenery every summer. She didn't mind school but had never really excelled. She found herself instead spending most of her time inside, reading about the world and smoking. Absentmindedly Anna would blow her little clouds of smoke through a screen, out into the intense beauty of her surrounding nature.

Food was central to her family's structure and identity. Her mother cooked continually and seemed very content blending a strangely delicious assortment of Eastern spiced rices, meat, curries, and soups with Western-style favorites. When prodded as to why they always ate at home, Anna's mother would say, "To eat anywhere else doesn't make any sense! We enjoy all the same things as the restaurants, except I make them healthier and with love. You will all miss my cooking when you leave me!"

This was enough of a guilt trip to keep everyone quiet and for the better part thankful. Anna's family consisted of herself, her mother, her father, her sister, her two younger twin brothers, her mother's ma and pa (who were ancient and required a lot of care), and her father's older sister, who also functioned like a grandparent. No matter what was served, at least one of the nine would be displeased, so even Anna had to agree with her mother's logic regarding going out to restaurants. In fact, she couldn't imagine how they would ever have afforded such a luxury.

The family ate breakfast together every morning, by which time her father had already been at work for hours. In the evening, when her father returned, everyone instinctively cleaned up and assembled once again for dinner. At this time her father, who spoke very rarely, would always say a basic grace. He would thank God for the wonderful food and the good health of everyone present, amen. Sometimes he would touch on one of the kids' achievements, which his wife would have briefed him on, and anyone who received such praise would radiate pride for the remainder of the meal. Everyone would then eat happily, and although the food was often quite good, their appetites were largely due to the fact that it was the second and the last time of the day that they would eat. This resulted in few leftovers—"Waste not, want not" was the common mantra.

Anna and her sister left home together a week after Anna graduated from high school, and they left permanently. It had become clear to the two grown girls in a house full of half-starved umpteenth generation Indians that the time for deadheading had come. Their twin brothers had somehow grown up ideally. They were social, athletic, and competitively brilliant. Anna's sister, Tilly, had saved up enough money working as an assistant at a legal firm to buy a roughly used electric car. Its potential for change overshadowed its tiny size, and a week after the purchase the two girls had packed. They finished bickering over what they each could bring, which amounted to little more than one traveling suitcase each, and then they took to the road. They left a very direct note to their family that sincerely thanked their parents and shared their love with their elders and their younger brothers. They finishing by saying that there was not enough in the region to keep them satisfied anymore and they needed to find out what was in store for their lives as individuals.

The girls had lied. They would have stayed if they felt they could have. There simply wasn't enough money or good work to allow them to stay comfortably in the place they loved with the people they loved dearly. The first two handwritten copies of their goodbye letter were thrown out because they felt the tear-smudged words would be too much for the family to bear. They needed a fresh page to leave behind. The last copy was typed, printed, and frustratingly packed wet, into a wet envelope. They left their cell phones and computers in boxes for the twins to use, with a note for each of the boys from each of the girls, saying *I Love You, Good Luck.*

Anna and Tilly cried for the majority of their first three hundred miles on the road. They escaped undetected after an unremarkable family dinner and found themselves arguing about their conviction after a day's drive. They tried and failed to sleep for the first few nights in the camouflage of mega-mart parking lots. If they avoided being frightened by the thieves and creeps of the night, they would end up finally drifting asleep as the sun began to set, wedged in the corners of their rigid seats. Each night they were told to leave by security guards, and they grew irritably exhausted nearly to the breaking point. On the third night they spotted an older security guard avoiding their area throughout the evening. They both finally slept for a few hours and just as the light of day first began to emulsify the horizon he firmly knocked on their window and told them in broken English that it was time to go. They thanked him for his blind eye, he said nothing more, and they carried on.

From that morning all the way through to the final day of driving together, Anna and Tilly grew bolder—more alert and more confident about their decision to leave. Anna had never seen her sister smile so much, and she aggressively beat at each sad, quiet moment with silly remarks and laughter. The feeling of freedom and adventure was contagious, and Anna began to join in on the fun as well. They discussed strategies for survival and discussed their wild plans for achieving love and happiness even against cold statistical odds. Anna had taken her life into her own hands and had never felt so powerful and wonderful. She knew that she had the ability to do anything she wanted for herself and, more importantly to her, the power to make things better for others.

In the city, Anna often worked for trade. Sometimes she would paint rooms in people's homes for clothes, food, and if she was lucky, a little cash. She didn't desire to be tracked by anyone. Her parents had a basic idea of where she lived, and she often wrote them loving emails. She was cautious, however, never to divulge any nonelectronic means by which anyone could contact her. She did not want to remain like this forever but had not found any kind of suitable employment that could support the lifestyle and flexibility she was able to eke out from odd jobs and hustling. She would be far too embarrassed to have her parents see how she lived and chose not to have them insist, as they would, on her moving home.

She was far from helpless, and she intended to stay that way. Anna was phenomenal at finding deals, couponing and generally taking advantage of any and all potential handouts, including free tampons and condoms from the soup kitchens and drop-in centers where she frequently volunteered her time. Her *not* being pregnant was essential to the freedom she desired in her young life. She was, however, happily sexually active with her boyfriend Aadir, whom she had met at a strange restaurant named

Cigarette's on a day they were offering half-price meals. Aadir had been an open book that day and they made a date to meet up again at Cigarette's. In the meantime, they couldn't refrain from texting continuously as they rode the waves of anticipation. After only one more of these meetings, Anna went home with Aadir. It certainly beat the women's shelter.

In the beginning, their relationship was something neither of them fully understood. Anna began to stay with Aadir more and more and eventually took her few personal items there as well. Although they indicated to each other that they were going to be monogamous, they didn't give up on the freedoms they'd enjoyed before meeting, and things seemed to be working brilliantly.

***

Anna sat across from Aadir in their favorite booth. They were chatting about trivial daily things, but Anna sensed that he was distracted and she had an idea of perhaps why.

"I need to say sorry for being gone so much, Aadir. I know we were spending a lot of time together and this seems like I am moving in a different direction, but I want you to know that this is not the case."

Aadir took a sip of his coffee and, for a second, looked a bit irritated. Then he exhaled and his face softened.

"Thanks Anna. I do trust you, of course. I guess I needed to hear that though. I know you have been busy with a couple painting gigs across the city and, to be honest, it's just nice that you continue to make the effort to keep coming back to this end so we can hang out."

Lately Anna had begun disappearing off and on, at odd times throughout the days, even sometimes spending the night at other friends' houses. She was making enough money to feel like a contributor but making it home late at night wasn't always an option. She had expected Aadir to panic, but he was really calm, and she appreciated the concerted effort.

"I know I have some abandonment issues going on, and although I try to ignore them it seems like I still need reassurance so I can relax."

Anna knew that Aadir had experienced loss in his life and that finding a balance between her own freedoms and his pathology would be a tricky line to walk. She needed the freedom to make quick decisions and take immediate action at this point in her life to ensure the survival and success of her new found independence.

"I had thought I would come to the city and be alone for a long time before I met someone I was interested in. You're super important to me already and just a cool cat overall, and I feel really lucky." She was smiling and hooked one of his feet under the table with her own.

He flipped the "he" to "we" dialogue right away. "We are pretty damn cool indeed," he said, leaning back deeper into his seat and twisting the curly hair that hung by his shoulders. "All the things I've ever loved have been a little challenging and unquestionably wonderful. And you are certainly wonderful."

Anna laughed, "You mean I am certainly challenging!"

Aadir smirked, "I said no such thing..."

Aadir fixated on Anna and she could see his eyes soften with relief; the distractedness of their earlier conversations had been banished by their confrontation, and they both felt pleasantly alive. They were both kind souls, grounded in sharing their strange lives together and growing outside of societal pressures as much as they could get away with in relative comfort.

Anna's feelings were growing strong enough in that moment that she desired to calm them down a bit. "I'm going to go for a puff, my dear," she told Aadir as she got up from her seat.

"Alright," Aadir replied, pretending to be indifferent and focusing back on the screen in front of him, his fingers moving wildly.

Anna walked toward the back door, passing by a couple she didn't recognize and she flashed them a small, closed-mouthed smile. She stepped outside and sat down on the scabby looking plastic chair. The local dog got up from where he was lying, and she lit her cigarette before beginning to pet him. Anna considered smoking her only real vice. She spent years filtering through dozens of brands and flavors until she found the kind of smoke that was lightest on her lungs while still packing the flavor and the buzz she enjoyed most. The actuality was that the taste she desired far outweighed any foreseeable health problems. For her, the experience centered on the feeling of "I do what I want." Which was her own cherished, childish control tactic.

Aadir hated her smoking more than anything she had ever seen him hate. She never smoked at home, other than the sheesha they took with Aadir's dad from time to time. But she also did not hide the fact that she smoked, that she smelled of smoke often, and was never found without a pack of emphysema rods. Heiress Ultra Lights were the prize and accumulation of her efforts, and she carried them in a tightly wrapped fold of glossy black fabric tied above the top of her pelvis. Since she had almost no hips whatsoever, she figured this addition gave her a healthier-looking feminine figure.

Aadir once called Anna's cigarettes "Power Sticks," and she refused to speak to him, making them both suffer through nearly two days of Aadir's apologetic pleadings. She eventually conceded that Aadir was right: smoking made her feel bigger, it made her feel present, it made her feel rebellious, but more than anything it somehow made her feel she was in control of her wild new life. She accepted that the artificial power the smokes gave her was real, and the health risks of her habit were also real, but she still made no effort to quit. Her puffs were short and deliberate, with a quick exhale. A far cry from the long and luxurious pulls one may see from some swaggering actor.

She stroked the dog's head beside her as she looked out at the gray but warm afternoon, thinking about all the cold days as an adolescent when she had lit incense and blown the smoke out of her window to keep her habit hidden. She had been going for walks before and after school to smoke, by herself mostly, since she turned thirteen. She had actually succeeded in never being caught by her parents, and that made her feel clever. The idea of hiding from Aadir never occurred to her, though. She had finally met someone who challenged her assumptions.

Patting the dog at her side she let her smoke hang idly in her other hand.

"Good boy, Cerberus," she said as she shook off some hair that had accumulated in her fingers.

The dog looked at her and closed his mouth for an instant. Then she resumed scratching his head, and he let his tongue hang out again. She casually had another drag and pushed the smoke out to join the rest of the murk in the sky outside. The trail of particulate dissipated into nothingness. There was something about this that always made her feel like any action she could take would be ultimately inconsequential.

"Okay, I'll see you later, handsome," Anna said to Cerberus as she bent the remaining half of her cigarette into a little jar of rocks until it was extinguished. She remained sitting for a moment longer, listening to the city around her. Cerberus nudged his muzzle under the hand she had placed on her lap and she was forced to pat him again, woken from her temporary, thoughtless bliss. "We're lucky people, Cerberus, you and I."

Chapter 4, Division

The Internet began its complete fundamental monitoring system in 2007. A new international policing system was established in 2034. Said to be an effective means of bringing down terrorists and pedophiles, the ideal behind the idea was presented as a godsent miracle. People around the world—those who were listening, anyway—were assured that this power was going to be under the careful eye of caring professionals. Many who heard the tearful applause of acceptance weren't convinced. Those with the real technical knowledge and the ability to understand what was actually happening were frightened and did their best to spread the potential threats of these controls, but to little avail.

The program was named Moses. The name pandered to the religious right wing but was still a fairly apt coinage, since it was supposed to split the murky seas of electronic criminal control. Instead of being a tool for caring safety watchdogs, however, multinational business conglomerates pressed their hands into Moses while the program was still warm. First-world governing bodies were then able to use citizens' tax dollars in the name of "national security," and suspicious activities of every kind became prevalent.

The sequential monitoring systems that were set up over those initial years were revolutionary. By tracking and scaling every web page viewed, every website created, and every word and picture uploaded or downloaded, Moses was effectively able to predict and segregate behavior and trends around the world. More importantly, the central nervous systems of people's most current weaknesses, ignorance, and fears were being exposed. This information was incredibly valuable, and the value of the companies tied into the initial investments soared above the imaginable.

Using baffling 3D nanotechnology in the 2030s, man created the means of storing information to the infabyte. The yottabyte—a trillion, trillion bytes (or if one prefers a million, billion gigabytes)—was now dwarfed by its impossible-seeming byte brother, who was a trillion times larger still. Technology had for the first time surpassed humanities capacity to use it. More importantly, through the research and development process, a super system of monitoring this information was created. It was a lot like creating an almost infinitely large storage locker for electronic information while having the foresight to make its walls completely transparent for viewing all of its contents.

The infabyte was championed in a facility of science-fictional size in the northern wastelands of Texas. It was surrounded by electrified wire and patrolled by armored vehicles with turret guns. Rumors of huge underground missile silos were not without merit. For those with influence it was an unlimited source of data. You could literally search the word "cola" and have hundreds of pages of graphs, statistics, and comparisons breaking down the word's use regionally and around the world. Then you could have it further broken down into any other data it was possibly correlated with. You could pinpoint every house that had ever typed the word *cola*, for any reason, onto a file or social network of any kind. There would be thousands of accessible pages of information neatly referenced in any preset manner that the user chose.

Codes were the next trend to overwhelm the Internet and thereby require more government funding to crack down on the apparently ingenious violent criminals. People found ways to pull the wool over "the eye of the internet" through encrypting and then decrypting their information. Instead of the heroism of web policing materializing, what instead happened was the location and closure of more websites and conversational feeds than ever in history. The free exchange of progressive and controversial ideas was being destroyed while credible distribution paths of camouflaged propaganda were succeeding in confusing their intended audience.

There were nearly two hundred jails in California and Texas alone, housing close to one-and-a-half million people, twenty percent of whom were convicted of Internet-related crimes. Many of the convicted were in actuality threatening the elite with their ideas and actions and benefiting the masses; these individuals were often surprised when they were rewarded with incarceration. For several years, the United States had been flirting coyly with imprisoning one in every hundred of its citizens. The country's debt was as insurmountable as the piles of cash in the grasping hands of private industry that were profiting off building and maintaining cages for human beings. Yet people generally continued on without much fuss, regardless of whether they were aware of this fact.

Anna's father's adoptive father was among the groups of people who had resisted the technological eye. For years people protested the policing of their private electronic habits, but in the end the power was not in their control. Anyone resisting was told that they were a member of a violent, perverse, criminal minority subclass. There were beatings and disappearances, but for the most part threats were effective enough to quell voices of disapproval. When Anna's grandfather was threatened that his adopted son and daughter might be removed from a house full of "incest child rapists," he buckled. He and his wife retreated to their home to take care of their family and ignored the problems of a future world that would be forced to exist without their participation.

***

Erecting a wall between the United States and Mexico had been proposed for over a hundred years. This proposal moved from drunken, ignorant ramblings to visceral reality when the Peace Border began its construction in 2051. It wasn't a conventional wall that was settled on, however. It was a virtual wall. The idea of a continuous physical wall was always silly. But when Israel proposed a contract to create a super network, managing the two thousand kilometers of border, it was passed by Congress and work began.

There were now twenty heavily guarded and heavily armed mega-towers strategically erected approximately every hundred miles. Unmanned armed patrol drones with advanced night vision flew between the towers in a seemingly sporadic pattern, and the men in the control rooms had the authority to "take evasive and, if necessary, lethal action against any criminals attempting to unlawfully infiltrate or smuggle into the United States of America." Simply saying "Shoot anyone entering the United States unconventionally" would not have sounded very good to a population not far removed from so many other countries, especially Mexico.

The division lines across the United States grew wider and more plentiful every year. Crime flourished in the potential of the voids as they were exposed. The separation was not just state-to-state, but the severe struggles of Irvine Texas, and Detroit Michigan, were outstanding case examples of full-level squalor and out of control crime. Some cities had overcome major obstacles and prospered, despite an initially bleak outlook. New

York still flourished, and the incredible tidal energy diking system that had been pioneered there—by American citizens, nonetheless—resonated around the world. A bustling cultural metropolis that created more energy than it consumed was born.

Each city, regardless of its successes or impoverishments, was heavily divided within itself. This was evident from the juxtaposition of visible fires in the wretched slums viewed from patios clinging to the sides of breathtaking, green, new age architectural buildings. Some of the public spaces, complete with volunteer tended gardens and floating boardwalks that lit themselves from the energy they produced, were keen examples of cooperation and innovation. These of course were only found in the wealthier public forums that were technically open to everyone but were policed by men armed with automatic weapons and defensive electrified billy clubs. Children of well-off parents mocked the officers and played them into their games in the splendid parks. Meanwhile, children in the same city's ghettos cowered in holes at every passing utterance of the word "Cops!"

Many of the disenfranchised citizens and much of the lazier media tended to confuse the *financial* and *political* collapse of America with the *collapse* of America. The country itself never actually altered its independence in the sense of a visual entity that all but the most impoverished children in the world could locate easily on a globe. All the individual states and lands still existed, with the exception of the lesser known American Samoan and Northern Mariana Islands, whose limited interests were absorbed by the Chinese to counter some of the United States' massive debt. All the remaining states still existed as fun shapes on classroom maps, where American children could approach them like unfamiliar prospective friends.

Residents who existed happily in the bowels and extremities of both excommunicated islands were sometimes unaware of the change in their ruling body until years after the transfer, and not a lot changed in the newly Chinese jurisdictions. In the remaining America, even fewer people noticed the loss of the islands, and the American lifestyle still *felt* similar to most, as they were told it had always been. The flag and anthem remained the same, and the sense of solidarity never faltered. In every state, tired schoolkids were once again required to mumble through pledging allegiance to the flag every morning, and you almost never saw a housing complex without several American flags noosed proudly in the front windows.

The deepening impoverishment of the nation strengthened a sense of unity within the massive exploding population blender. The blacks, Mexicans, Asians, and Middle Easterners who'd been scapegoated for generations weren't seen by frustrated whites as "stealing" anyone's jobs anymore. There were no jobs, anyway. The word "job" insinuated something purposeful and perhaps desirable. Now there were only the odd openings for grinding menial labor in hazardous areas or suicidal paper-shuffling in tiny cubicles smudged from years of breathless people leaning on their walls.

Honky, cracker, or whitey weren't seen by frustrated minorities as "keeping them down" anymore, either. Corporations had grown entirely faceless and enjoyed dangling aggressively employed equal-opportunity representatives and spokespeople in front of anyone who questioned their methodical irresponsibility. Each race was respectively ashamed of its own examples of unelected ambassadors pandering to the ignorant. Most people went about their daily tasks of working and sleeping or stealing and scheming. Throughout the day, few people meandered much further than a block or two, usually to eat, before returning home to familiarity. This was life.

People essentially faced fewer and fewer choices. It was a common perception that drug abuse was the most rampant it had been in all of history, but the rate per capita had remained relatively intact for decades. Drug abuse and its consequences and filthy realities were forced into the public's daily senses because of the epidemic of the roaming homeless and the partially sheltered. Also, higher quality drugs such as refined cocaine, real MDMA, psilocybin and LSD were almost unheard of due to their cost and because of the difficulty of their acquisition. The percentage of people who would have been recreational users of these products were now replaced by far more addled and addicted wretches huffing industrial wastes and drinking everything from cleaning products to hairspray.

The majority of the public were terrified of these dusty, hunched creatures who slept quietly beneath their stairwells after late nights of screaming themselves to tears in the streets. They were also content with their belief in their president, who had supposedly spent every available moment of the last three years working on "The Eradication of Drugs by a United America." Concerned citizens felt the sense of an increasingly united America, so the drug problem seemed to be under control. They could now look at the ever-growing piles of huddled homeless people through eyes certain that their bothersome daylight snoozes were numbered—certain that the trails of vomit and piss would dry up when their bodies dematerialized, and certain that their previous resting spots would soon sprout wildflowers.

Chapter 5, Help Yourself

Cynthia stood at the entrance to the decrepit house and rang the doorbell. She heard no movement coming from inside, and for a moment she stared passively at the uneven and cracked concrete chunk on which she stood.

"Come on ..." she said under her breath as she looked behind her to see a man walking by and looking in her direction. She hadn't worn a costume today because this patient's house was so close to her own. She began to feel naked and foolish for her incautious laziness. She rang the buzzer again, and almost immediately someone opened the door. They must have crept silently to the entranceway and were likely assessing her through the peephole, making their decision of whether to open up.

"Did you order some assistance?" Cynthia asked the stout, uncertain-looking lady who stood in front of her. This opening sentence had been specifically chosen as a vague introduction for these encounters. If she had arrived at the wrong house or someone had a change of heart, she could easily say, "Oh, I'm sorry, must have the wrong address," and the stranger could be left to assume whatever they wanted of her.

The nameless lady caught on quickly. "Yes, I did. Come in please."

Cynthia wasted no time getting inside and closing the door behind her. She felt some semblance of relief.

"My son is this way," the nervous lady said, and she took off down the hallway toward a room at the end.

Cynthia understood her urgency but needed to be consistent in her approach.

"I'm sorry I have to be so abrupt, ma'am, but I take payment first. It is just the nature of things, I hope you understand."

The lady stopped quickly enough that one of her shoes made a squeak on the floor. She spun around and said, "Yes, of course. One moment," before running into the kitchen to find her purse.

Cynthia looked around quickly and followed her. The lady handed her a bundle of dog-eared bills with a hair elastic tied around it.

"It's all there, I assure you."

Cynthia forced a smile and said, "I trust you and thank you. Now let's go see your son."

The young man who she had come to assess was lying in bed, winching in pain. His face was pale and unwashed looking. He had been sweating. His arm lay on his chest wrapped in a rag covered in red-and-brown bloodstains. He was gripping the bloody rag around his arm so tightly that the veins on his hand bulged.

"What happened here?" Cynthia asked.

"They were trying to jump between two buildings, and he fell onto a car," the mother answered for her son.

The son flinched a bit as Cynthia began wrapping a tourniquet around his skinny bicep. She then removed his bloody rag and some dark blood oozed onto his pants. The crimson stream slowed quickly. She felt the arm gently.

"Uh, I see we have a break here, but it isn't too major. Do you have any allergies?" Cynthia asked the boy.

"Not that I know of," he answered, without providing Cynthia any assurance.

"He doesn't," his mom said.

"Okay. I'm going to numb the area," Cynthia said, with the needle already in the teen's arm. He didn't react to the pinprick.

"Have one of these, too." She handed him a heavy painkiller, and before she could explain what it was or give him any water it was down the hatch. Things were going better than usual, and she was ready to begin stitching within two minutes of meeting her patient.

She threw the old rag on the ground among a pile of mismatched sports pads and some old flak gear. One of the strangest recent trends gaining momentum was kids wearing body armor. Far too many children and parents had given in to their fears of the outside world and doomed their obese families to an indoor electronic cocoon. But as long as there were human beings there would always be adolescents with the aim of pushing limits and challenging preconceptions, and eventually there came a generation who rejected video games and indoor family time.

Videos all over the Internet of kids ignoring caution and venturing out into the streets and woods to find adventure began going viral. The most common associated hashtags were #gearingup, #getgearedup and #frontierkids. Schoolkids who participated acquired leather clothes, motocross vests, gloves, and sports padding, and they wore them underneath loose-fitting clothes in an ironic attempt to defy being confined. The young man with the mangled arm lying in front of Cynthia was one of these brats.

Cynthia didn't want to spend an instant longer than necessary in the stranger's home, so she checked to see that the broken arm was set with a hand over the boy's mouth protecting both his mother and any neighbors from the scream. She thought it unfortunate that the flexing of childhood freedoms so often had painful results. At least this new trend was getting the kids away from screens for a bit. It was a strange trade-off. Concerned parent groups had been posting their videos and sharing memes to urge other parents and kids to take a stand against this dangerous behavior. This response seemed to work counterintuitively. Kids who kept pushing their own physical limits exploded, and people began getting hurt with no means of paying for health care. As always, new problems created new solutions though, and ten years after health care was repealed a new system that went by the name Doctors Without Order had been established.

Cynthia had been a Doctor Without Order for five years and had seen the country's mismanaged health-care facilities worsen during this time. The demand for care was being alternatively satisfied. People silently prided themselves on knowing someone who knew someone, and by trading favors, or by surrendering more cash than they would have liked, a person in the market for real aid could receive a visit. The visit would always come from a stranger, who would drop in at a somewhat unscheduled time. The patients would not have the luxury of establishing a trusting relationship with their potential savior during these distressing situations. Their personal security had to be temporarily suspended for a chance of receiving the help they needed. It was a nerve-racking game for both the patients and the practitioners.

Cynthia completed the stitches in the boy's arm as he watched intermittently. She then mixed two gooey liquids together on a piece of flat cardboard. She kneaded them with her gloved hands and began wrapping the compound around the boy's arm. After this she sprayed a fine mist from a small clear bottle over the area, and the cast changed to a white color as the solution hardened.

"Alright, we are all done here," Cynthia said to the air, addressing neither the mother nor the son. "I'm assuming you don't have the money to pay for this accident, do you?" She asked the boy as she removed her surgical gloves.

"No," he said quietly, as he wiggled his fingers. His previous angst appeared to be all but extinguished. He looked much younger now and had the uncertainty of a lost pup.

Cynthia continued as she packed up her few instruments and other products into her purse. "Well, your mom barely does either. I'm in a position now to give you some advice, and I will take the opportunity to do so. Use your brain. Don't do stupid things that will undermine your family's foundation." She pointed to the pads on the ground. "I like that you and your friends are creating a more active generation, but let the other kids be the guinea pigs, alright?"

The kid looked at her and said, "Ya."

He was clearly embarrassed, but his mother must have done something right in raising him because after a moment, and unprompted by his mom, he said, "It's just frustrating. I don't want anything to do with anything that is sold to me. I hate electronics; everyone just touches screens and keys until they die. I want to live and feel like I am doing something worthwhile."

Cynthia found this statement uplifting. Her own son had once shared a similar zealousness. She was surprised that the boy was confiding in her, so she continued her lecture.

"Treating yourself, your family, and others well is something very worthwhile. If you continue to do this you will begin to discover what you are truly passionate about, and you will end up finding and doing what you love. If you continue to tear yourself apart you will have tossed away all the precious energy you have right now."

Cynthia turned to the boy's mother, and added, "I certainly wish I still had that much fire left!"

The lady chuckled and smiled. Her face was colorful with relief. She had her hands clasped together, and it looked like she was fighting the urge to hug Cynthia. "Thank you," she said.

Cynthia nodded.

As she left she closed the door behind her and glanced again at the decaying front stoop, stepping over the largest of the cracks filled with dirt and bits of blue plastic. She began her walk home, reflecting on the boy who was recently sewn up and wishing for him to believe in what she had told him. She knew that life for a teenager didn't often feel easy since she had raised two of her own children through their teenage years and remembered how challenging the rate of changes were. The world was now a place with more visible contradictions than ever, and she knew now that all these struggles persisted into adulthood. The only real difference was that a person became more used to them as they aged and more equipped to stay rational as they were being bludgeoned into decision-making. The choice needed to be made whether to submit or resist, and the outcome of each choice was a gamble.

Marginally successful, labor-intensive proprietary businesses were one of the few viable options for anyone looking to earn a sense of everyday control within their limited world. Those who ventured into non-computer-based businesses that depended on their physical capabilities, such as construction and restaurant ownership, were willing to risk injury for the potential return of financial freedom. These were seriously dangerous occupations, though, and hospitals had become terrifying places. Fewer than forty percent of American citizens earning at or below the national average income had health insurance, and even those who were covered ran the risk of losing their life savings trying to stay alive when misfortune drove its poisoned teeth into their naked flesh. Everyone tried their best to be careful and, as always, life ran its course as a labyrinth with sharp edges.

But risk averse behavior was growing more dangerous all the time as well. Folks who obsessed about their well-being were so paranoid and jittery that they found themselves distracted and clumsy. Simple flubs like dropping tools and slipping in kitchens often resulted in lacerations, broken bones, hysteria, pain, panic, death … This was an unfortunate reality in times of uncertainly. The spectacle of deterioration was experienced and witnessed enough that it added sparks to gloomy people's combustible clouds of conviction. Those individuals who, on a day-to-day basis, were generally afraid, often had to look no further than their own tired-eyed reflections in a teaspoon to find their greatest threat.

Even those who did end up surviving a hospital stay, young or old, emerged feeling a little older and more jaded than when they were admitted. Life bullied those who believed that the pull of their grief magnetically attracted pity. There was something inherently repulsive about adults who exhibited infantile characteristics. Instead of coddling their cries, agitated nurses would usher these squeaky wheels out of the hospitals with painkillers to ease their undoubted transition into worse places. Injured people found themselves courting the borders of depression as they sorted through the catastrophic information available to them on the Internet set there to further confuse their situation and to sell them something. After struggling to self-diagnose their disorders with little avail, disappointed citizens would search for answers as to why the system operated the way it did. A wall awaited at the end of their alley of questions, and it appeared as the unscalable, staggering magnitude of the health-care problem that towered over the insignificance of their own experiences.

Contacting the DWO (Doctors without Order) was generally viewed as a risky option, but often enough they were the only option. Cynthia enjoyed what she did, and even though her colleagues were the subjects of a rash of controversy they were also unquestionably saving lives. Most of the DWO shared a similar story. In their adolescence the aspiring medics had dreamed of becoming real doctors as they lay under their cold sheets. The children who became real doctors alternatively dreamed of toys in large, colorful private bedrooms. The DWOs essentially playing doctor in their adulthood were not witch doctors, and they did have organized meetings, mostly online. Private forums were held where they discussed medicine, but they had no government-recognized certifications, and the risks were almost unlimited.

Only the highest echelon practitioners actually performed surgery, and most of these individuals were ex-surgeons to begin with. The majority of DWO visits involved basic patch-ups and simple diagnoses. They depended on word-of-mouth to keep people as healthy and as alive as possible. If they were fully dedicated, an individual quack could be responsible for the preservation of thousands of lives over a career, many of whom received only one visit. This ungovernable system was surprisingly efficient. Less surprisingly, traditionalists were supremely freaked out.

Those who favored population control through "the natural order of things" loathed the DWO, and there were casualties because of this dispute. An actual delivery person who was gunned down by a suspicious, self-righteous vigilante brought the DWO's existence to its political height. The media showed the image of a poor surprised girl lying beside her plastic-wrapped bouquet of flowers, surrounded by a halo of blood. The news media condemned the DWO as murderers and demanded a representative step forward and be held accountable. No one ever emerged to do so, and people continued to receive help from the

DWOs during this period, even if potential new patients were far less likely to be considered because of the heat.

The memory of this event was still fresh in Cynthia's mind, and it had replaced some of the joy she took from her daily work with paranoia. She had walked a haphazard route on the way home and even stopped at a convenience store to break up the journey and check for followers. They had recently taught her these tactics at a DWO e-conference. She browsed some magazines and bought a chocolate bar but became frustrating with the time she was wasting and continued on. Upon returning home she immediately locked the door behind her. A weighty sigh escaped her lungs as she sat down on her little wooden entranceway chair to take her shoes off. Cynthia placed her shoes beside her medical bag, which was really just a cheap purse, and stared at a picture of her younger self standing between her son and daughter enjoying the view of a picturesque lake.

How much longer can I do this? she wondered. The picture on the wall made her happier, and her fatigue waned. She took out her cell phone and looked at the time. Loneliness washed over

her.

Where the hell is Will? She wanted her husband home now.

He was late. Again.

Chapter 6, Tea

Even though his shift had been over for nearly an hour, Sheriff William was still in his uniform. He had robotically wrapped up his paperwork early, and he decided to stop by Cigarette's for a break before heading home to his wife. A cup of strong tea always had a way of evening him out, and he felt this was a good way of bringing more of himself and less of his pain back to Cynthia. The warmth of the tea made him feel younger and relaxed his nerves. The earthy flavors kept him grounded. Each session reminded him of his mother's relentless optimism. She had always told him that, "Even though sometimes it may not feel like it, remember: every effort and kindness you bless the world with turns into pure love and hope. You are creating something out of nothing, William." He had seen many of his efforts over the years blossom with blinding colors. On the other hand, he had seen so much suffering that it seemed like too few people were trying at all.

Immediately after starting his night shift the day prior, William had been called to a scene where the driver of a garbage truck had found a dead man and woman leaning together behind a trash bin. The rest of the evening and morning he had been very quiet, allowing the discovery's image and the heavy insinuations to continue processing in his head without respite. He guessed that they were likely still teenagers, but it could be hard to tell with addicts. They'd both died with their eyes partially open above filthy, vomit-stained shirts. As he sat on the plush seat of his booth sipping his tea, thoughts kept circling in his mind, and he was finding few answers: How many years of meaningless suffering and neglect did these two endure before being driven to this type of self-destruction? How could people with what seemed like no concern for anything end up like that, together? Had either of them even had a chance to experience the embrace of kindness and happiness in their short lives?

The sheriff cycled through his bleak considerations and was stirring around some of the tea leaves in the bottom of his cup when Chef Josef sat down uninvited, as he often did. William sighed heavily, offering a cue to Josef that he hadn't ordered any conversation. If Josef had noticed William's stoic, closed-off body language it appeared that he didn't care. William had wanted only to meditate on the tragedy silently over a few cups of tea and then head right home to Cynthia. It was clear that Josef wanted to talk, however, and since initiating conversation was something rarely seen from the chef, William put his troubles aside to lend a friendly ear to his comrade's problems.

"How's the tea, Will?" Josef asked.

"It's always different and always wonderful," William responded to the token question. He was trying to be pleasant, but his usually powerful voice was not much more than a mutter.

"I know," Josef replied, taking a long sip of something from a dingy silver container that William presumed to be coffee.

"We do a good job here ... We do." The chef looked out the window with his hands clasped. "That bastard health inspector, though, Will. He comes by here every other fucking day now."

The word *fuck* came out fluently when the chef spoke it. The words *health inspector* made William more uncomfortable than the profanity.

"Maybe if he'd just *have* a cup of tea or something, he could be as cool as a cup of…" The chef seemed to lose his train of thought. "Of … whatever … like you?"

William saw that Josef was looking for a reaction to what Josef no doubt thought was a generous compliment.

His statement barely made sense, but William got the gist of it. Josef scratched his head, visibly irritated. William let the silence settle for a moment and had another sip of his hot tea. He knew Josef wanted to vent a bit more, and at this point the less William interjected the quicker he would be able to make an exit.

"Jesus, maybe my sauces are health hazards," Josef continued, sounding a little exhausted. "But I wouldn't brew the stuff in my *special* little *sinks* if I could make it in my kitchen, in the open, like a civilized son of a bitch."

Josef spit these words out like acid, referring to the dozens of small containers where he kept his creations. He literally hid these in various places around the restaurant. He once let slip to William that, in addition to most of them being located in a secret crawl space, one of the other hiding places was a pull-out drawer under his bed. This bed was where he and Steven slept, in a room above the restaurant. William had earned Josef's trust and had thereby known for years about what seemed to him to be an innocent breach of code in a world with so many more graphic, violent problems.

"Well, maybe all that mess you and Steven make upstairs after hours adds the character to our meals that keeps us all so equally satisfied?"   Sheriff William returned this snarky, adolescent comment while looking up from blowing on his tea with an unforced smirk.

The chef chuckled in spite of himself for a moment, still looking mostly out the window. "Ah well, I guess. It's essentially the same as the bed-sauce at all the other food spots. Perhaps my sex powers really do make all the difference! No. I'm not even that good at that … but I do make great sauces. I'm terrific at that."

The chef was successfully distracted from his grief, and William was satisfied with this accomplishment.

The chef continued, looking at the sheriff now. "The secret is aging. Unlike sex." He then exploded with a few short but loud laughs. It was contagious, and William chuckled a bit as well.

"*Hey*!" Josef's tone changed suddenly. "And keep that bedroom talk in your own head. Hey, *cop*?" He turned back from the interior of the restaurant and stared straight at the unfazed sheriff.

"I should have you settle your tab up right now and have my Steven smack the crap out of you! He's a lot feistier than he looks!" Josef's thoughts began to move quickly now. "I'm not even supposed to keep tabs? What if you started running off somewhere, well, what the shit? And my Steve? You're talking about my husband now? We're sitting here talking about my husband? I *never* talk about your wife. I never even talk about me and Steve. I hope you're not gay-bashing all of a sudden, and you know…"

William decided to cut off the tangent. "Look, Josef with an 'eff', relax. We're talking about sauce." He lured the conversation from the darkness with the distraction of a sound of "eff". It was a strange but effective diversion.

Those snickering children and arrogant adults who possessed flagrant ideas of what it meant to be a homosexual male all assumed that the *f* in Josef's name was a cosmetic personal upgrade. Backing up this theory was the fact that every shirt he wore had Chef Josef written in cursive on the upper left-hand side. Steven had the same style of text on his work shirts, and his was followed by a little red heart. The extra stitching *was* a bit flamboyant, but Steven always told anyone who pried that "Since servers can't have sleeves, I had to wear my heart somewhere!" Both men were proud of who they were, but Josef chose to carry the sin of his pride quietly. Except when it came to his cooking.

Josef smiled at William's reference to his work. "Good. I like to talk about sauces, because my sauces are the *'eff'ucking best.* The absolute, fucking, best."

***

Cynthia knew William's tea habit intimately. She appreciated his transitional attempts, even if it meant occasionally waiting an extra hour or two before he arrived home. She also knew exactly where he would be having his tea and with whom he would be talking. Even in his late fifties, William was a large and strong presence. People gravitated to him. His massive toned shoulders and arms were situated symmetrically above a lean torso, and his smile was transparently kind. Sometimes his overwhelming demeanor left people searching vacantly for things to say, and this proved most effective when he was on the job. They had been married for more than twenty years, and Cynthia still caught herself rambling now and then.

Cynthia knew she was pretty but always felt less physically attractive than William. She felt that her empathy, intelligence, and transcendent spirituality were her strong suits. She could walk through a crowd of dozens of people, and catch half of them just needing to take a second look at her as if they were sensitive to her unique blend of energies. Animals were always drawn to her as well and would stare at her inquisitively or become quieted with her presence.

When William was at his lowest she nearly always found a way to calm him and convince him that perhaps humanity had potential and purpose after all. She knew in her heart that their love was strong, but she could never shake the irrational feeling that some beautiful young harlot would somehow manipulate William and steal everything Cynthia cared about away from her. She had met women who'd tried to have William before, but each time she saw these efforts shatter against a wall of William's calm, head-shaking reality.

Nevertheless, Cynthia had followed William two or maybe five times when he began coming home up to an hour after she knew he was done work. He had told her over the preceding few weeks about some sick man who had been methodically killing elderly women and then staying in their empty apartments. He also told her in a wavering voice that the man had been linked to over a dozen homicides of this nature, and that this number was expected to grow. Both Cynthia and William were deeply upset by this gruesome inhumanity, and their days together during this time were full of somber moments.

It was then that Cynthia noticed William's behavior changing in addition to his later arrivals home. He was more irritable than she had ever known him to be, and he would often lash out in frustration when he ran out of words to say. It seemed to Cynthia that he was avoiding her, as if her very presence upset him. When she finally grew angry enough to wait outside the precinct to follow William after work, she had prepared herself to find him with some gorgeous, young, morally deprived whore and had filled herself with hatred. The only thing Cynthia discovered during her shadowing was that Will would sit in a strange restaurant called Cigarette's. Without him ordering anything, a little pot of tea would be delivered to him, and sometimes he would chat with the oddball owners of the place, but more often he would sit alone and drink his tea. Once she'd watched him consume two entire pots before preparing to leave.

Before this episode involving what the Internet was calling "the octogenarian axer," he had usually come home from rough cases in a somewhat defeated fashion, and it was Cynthia who'd brewed him tea. These days became very predictable. Nearly everything would frustrate him for the first several hours after his arrival, and unless she could somehow dance around his moodiness, both of them would lose sleep due to strung-out emotions. Still, she felt a little betrayed that he was having his tea elsewhere … until she noticed the change. When he came home after breaking for tea at Cigarette's she felt drawn to him like she had decades ago. He was happy, calm, and full of powerful grace.

They made love more often. They made love with the vigor of eager adults and would then lie down soiled and without any care to be elsewhere or to think of what came next. Their life seemed once again as if it was their own to enjoy.

Cynthia was thrilled when eventually William took her to Cigarette's. After a few months they began to go once or twice a week. She loved it. They had always loved each other powerfully, but their lives once again seemed more fluid and enjoyable. After a few surprisingly delicious dinners, Cynthia felt the need to come clean.

"Will … these last few weeks have been just incredible. I love that we are doing things together again and I am having so much fun." She stopped for a moment and took a deep breath, preparing herself for what she planned to say. She felt like it might end the winning streak they were on, but she revered honesty too much to keep things from her husband.

"I followed you a few times over the last several weeks after work, to see where you were going. I know that I should have simply trusted you or asked you where you were, and I know it was ridiculous for me to have done so, but we were struggling to speak at the time, and I just didn't know what else to do. I got carried away, and I'm really sorry, Will."

William took a butter knife and used it to gather a little pile of sauce from the leftovers on his plate before popping it in his mouth to savor.

"I know," William said.

"You know what?" replied Cynthia. "You know I'm sorry?" She was confused and a little irritated at William for not taking the situation more seriously.

"I know you were following me, Cynthia," William said as he leaned forward and looked straight into her eyes. "If anyone needs to apologize, it is probably me. I was acting way out of line for a few weeks, maybe even a few months there, and I never gave you any explanation as to why. You had the right to be suspicious because we have an open and honest relationship."

Cynthia felt relieved immediately. "I can't believe it! I thought I was being so careful! You must be a pretty decent officer after all, Will, because I am stealthy like a bloody leopard."

They both chuckled. Cynthia couldn't help but enjoy these conversations that reinforced their love for one another over the years. She also couldn't have cared less about William letting her stew in guilt for her behavior. It was the future that concerned her the most.

"I've known and shared with you every high and low of our lives, and no matter what, I can handle them all as long as you let me know what's going on. I really mean that, Will; there is nothing you could say to me that would make me love you any less. You just need to let me know what you are going through, okay?"

William failed to respond for a second, and Cynthia could see that he was thinking. So she repeated herself to let him know that she really meant what she said.

"Okay? You need to tell me when something serious is bothering you." She reached out and squeezed his massive hand as hard as she could and shook it a little, as if to drive her

conviction into him.

"Okay," William replied, with what appeared to be a mixture

of relief and difficulty. "I will certainly always try."

Chapter 7, Inside Cigarette's

Most entrepreneurs were lacking in even the most basic accounting and management skills. In addition to this, many were driven by a skewed concept of business. They often took out exorbitant loans in order to reap what they predicted to be the greatest rewards offered to them for their bold acceptance of risk. Then they went bankrupt.

Even if they dodged the snares of ignorance, roaming regulatory snipers were always eager to administer fines. After the fines were collected, somewhere, pods of horrid human parasites spent their time narrowing regulations. They did their best to steal any breath of spirit from people more creative than themselves who were attempting something incomprehensibly outside the black-and-white spectrum of a checklist. These agencies hid the fact that they overlooked the nation's atrociously rotting public facilities while enforcing unrealistic standards on private efforts.

The discouraging reality of these organizations was hidden behind soft, inviting logos and acronyms promising to protect the health of an indifferent general public and a few screaming alarmists.

Cigarette's was a drawer full of mismatched utensils; splendid individuals all with an inherent purpose. As a unit, however, a practical individual with a matching orthodox replacement set may simply discard them due to their lack of conformity. But utensils are stubborn things and the quality of the individual far outweighs the continuity of the set. If you look deep enough into nearly every home you can find an old utensil independent of its brethren usually cherished because of its effectiveness regardless of the way it looks.

Cigarette's was originally given its name by its chain-smoking forebear Albert Szekely. He had purchased what at the time had been a vegan restaurant and decided to create a throwback southern steakhouse. He loved meat and smoking more than anything else and to the horror of his critics continued to live with these vises until a ripe old age. He spent most of the development budget for Cigarette's on the smoking room as a tribute to his passions. The project drew a lot of local attention. The room was, in fact, compliant with all regulations, yet it defied everything common to every other smoking room that had been created before it. Confounding to Albert, his over-compliance with the laws actually set the stage for a regulatory hook to drive into his restaurant's veins. Some of the powers that be were irked by the strangeness of the facility and were awakened from their despicable slumber.

The smoking room set up was hyper-space-aged bravado that literally took the entrants' breath away. Massive silent hood fans gently stole the tobacco smoke so desperately sought after and enjoyed by its users, only to blow it away above the buildings outside. The light was somehow uplifting but not overbearing and came from a multitude of sources leaving an absence of shadows, which was impressive for the windowless smoking space. Catchy dated songs with repetitive choruses were leaked out of hidden speakers that seemed to be everywhere. The fans alone were costly, but they were necessary to satisfy regulations. This expense had to be budgeted for by every new restaurant owner looking to have their own smoking room. In accordance with the tradition of overdoing it though, Albert had doubled the required number of fans and had each of them dipped in chrome.

The shiny turbines and other trivial amenities added up quickly, but what really doomed the original Cigarette's was the amount of time and money spent on the gorgeous, meticulously crafted, asymmetrical carved hardwood wall panels. The man who created them had been a lifelong friend of Mr. Szekely's, and at the time Albert had had cash to blow. With impossible depth and detail the hermit artist slowly pulled away layer upon layer of wood, exposing his imagination. This irregularity had immediately infuriated officials. They had condemned the effort after its initial inspection, saying that the angular wood surfaces presented both a fire hazard and a safety concern for people leaning against them.

Mr. Szekely was not swayed. He decided to hire another eccentric artist aching to use a relatively new portable smelting technology. Liquid aluminum was sprayed a quarter of an inch thick, covering all three dimensions of the room. The spectacle worked seamlessly and baffled inspectors. Other than the large invisible door, which had a thin stream of circulated air blowing directly upward from its lower void, there were no breaks in the incredible four aluminum walls and the floor. The invisible door negated the need for other emergency exits because it was the size of three standard doorways. Pressurized air was thrust up and its ceiling-ward motion was never broken as a slow-moving turbine pulled the air the rest of the way up and out of Cigarette's into the grayness outside.

A person's feet would definitely feel uncomfortable if they dared to cross the opening shoeless. Most of the customers who had a chance to experience this unique brand of homeostasis felt slightly uncomfortable as they rushed through the portal, trying not to seem naive. By hair level the pull was barely noticeable. It was such an achievement of balance. The nonsmoking patrons even got to enjoy viewing the room of vice through the massive door of air but heard very little, since the air and fans muffled the conversations on opposing sides.

The business went bankrupt eight months after the smoking room's completion. It was a shame to waste all of the *free* publicity it had earned. Shortly after this, Albert was jailed for a hilariously long list of nearly every kind of embezzlement, evasion, theft, and forgery a person could contrive in order to cycle cash and credit. It was quite the feat to have created such an intricate mess. The man, the star, Albert Szekely, had been hyped all over the city when he went missing, and it took less than a week to find him. He was finally arrested on Tortola Island in the Caribbean. This desperate move to a tiny area was the most foolish and traceable thing he had done since his youth. Its silliness was proof of the mistake of aging.

From his hideout, Albert was quietly ushered back to his home city and toward his certain incarceration. He was just another rebel and, at the time, the media loved rebels so much that they had a new one to expose every few days. The authorities were sure Albert's appeal would fizzle quickly. They were wrong. Thanks to his charisma he had unexpected staying power. In fact he stayed in the spotlight for years after his incarceration, and students around the city wore shirts that read Szekely-Sized Balls.

What really drew the public into both following and discussing the spectacle was that the eighty-six-year-old man was seen smiling throughout the entirety of his trial. The ordeal was televised and was ridiculously long. Albert would make hilarious and often truthful testimony somehow without incriminating himself. He had a way of spinning words to his advantage and when necessary used bits of doublespeak better than even the most prepped of politicians. He was often threatened with contempt of court for chuckling to himself while the prosecution threw up their hands at evidence that was as easy to untangle and present as a ball of crushed barbed wire.

Albert Szekely died on the toilet, the evening after his conviction, alone in his cell. The officer who brought him his breakfast opened the cell door, initially thinking that Albert was either asleep or playing a joke. He was humiliated when he shook the man's shoulders and Albert plummeted off his roost half-naked with his ass pointing up in the air, certainly dead. The guard couldn't help himself and eventually leaked Mr. Szekely's final moments to the media. Those who were interested couldn't have been more satisfied. Whoever smuggled in the fatal dose of drugs that gave Albert a few intense instants of bliss before his quick death was never found.

***

As far as the restaurant's future was concerned, the banks needed to shell off the massive screaming symbol of loss as quickly as possible. It was purchased by Chef Josef Almos, one of only three bidders just a few weeks after the trial began. Josef had no interest in the fancy smoking room; he only had interest in cooking food, making a living, pleasing his husband, and being left alone. Immediately after receiving his entrance code for the abandoned building's front door he went to work. Some people came to see what he was doing with the place, which sparked such interest during the trial that his husband, Steven, told the inquiring public to come back soon for food worthy of the eccentric Albert.

When Josef first arrived he briefly inspected the bizarre three-room main floor of the commercial space. Then he began to set up a plan that had been in his mind prior to ever seeing what he had purchased. It was a massacre. Every secondary hood fan, was sold off for pennies on the dollar. Josef made waste out of nearly his entire personal toolbox and an investment of metal-ready blades, as he succeeded in clawing through loads of aluminum, bolts, and wood to reorganize the space.

There was a large doorway cut between the actual kitchen (that was slightly larger than the smoking room) and the smoking room itself. The torn and reshaped entranceway to the extended kitchen was professionally fireproofed a week later, right over the state-of-the-art smokescreen that had been a one-of-a-kind attraction. The outdated touch-screen tables used mostly for games and connectivity were ripped from within their silent smokeless masterpiece and then bolted to the dining area floor and surrounded by C-grade secondhand furniture and a few booths bought from another bankrupt restaurant a few blocks away. A dozen new touch-screen table mats had to be purchased for the fake wood grain booths that were placed against the front windows, but the rest of the restaurant was left the same. This included some things that Josef swore he would change if he ever had the money, such as the British racing green ceiling panels and other gimmicks that added to the feeling of misplacement.

Following the quick rearrangement, Chef Josef was satisfied that he had enough room to work. After the street sale of most of the knickknacks and collectables, he was satisfied that he had shed the weight of Cigarette's nostalgic past. With the help of an excited Steven, he then began getting the food logistics organized. In just over three months the couple opened their doors to the achievement of their bizarre and lovely dream. The facility was a gaudy place, and many people dismissed it after only peering in the windows from the street. Those who gave the new shop a fair shot, on the other hand, were pleased. People who enjoyed the banter with the owners and other frequent patrons were rewarded for their loyalty. They received good food, some of it illegal, and they had the simple joy of quality eating brought back into their lives. The customers preferred Cigarette's to their own apartments until they were full of good food and bothered enough by the enjoyment of the other patrons to return home. They purchased perspective. It was delicious.

Chapter 8, Ahead of the Idea

Josef's parents suspected that he was gay early in his childhood. He dressed up in his mother's clothes when he was left alone and was discovered more than once. He was only interested in the more flamboyant characters on his television shows and, to his mother's dismay, he kept insisting on painting his face and subsequently smudged it all over the house. Fortunately, neither of his parents minded the implications of their son's behavior and encouraged him to explore anything that made him happy, anything that could hold his young interest. What primarily held his interest as he grew was cooking and eating. This suited everyone else in the household, and by the age of nine Josef was already taking out meat to thaw in the morning so that when he returned from school it would be ready for culinary experiments. There was joy in their home. Josef identified with being gay and with being talented and with being loved, and never questioned himself.

The preferences of Josef's husband, Steven Havez, however, were not so clear to anyone. He was a striking, milky skinned, vaguely Latino boy and looked as polished as a thousand-dollar pen in a display case. His features, even from the age of four, sparked second and third takes from jealous mothers of slack-jawed, butter-faced, doughy brats. The idea of his sexuality was never addressed until he was in high school and found himself feeling nothing for the rich girls all his friends insisted were desirable. The girls took turns trying to lure him into romantic relationships. Each left a bit of her confidence behind in the wake of his rejection. A charmer from birth, he was apt to lead on girls even in his elementary classes, until his parents told him to stop, since he was "clearly too young for a girlfriend." In high school, while he was still leading a little lineup of babbling, insecure, lusty girls, his parents told him to stop since he was "clearly gay."

There were no tears or temper tantrums. Steven, feeling ashamed and lost, only said, "I'm sorry."

His mother replied sternly, "Don't be sorry for who you are, Steven, but we expect you to apologize for teasing Ellie."

Ellie was the girl who had been following him around and assuming she was his girlfriend at the time.

"And we expect you to be more considerate of others, Steven. We have taught you much better than that," his father summarized.

"Okay, I will be. I promise," was all Steven said, and he and his parents didn't really discuss his sexuality or its lack thereof ever again.

After his parents had presumably outed him, he was certain that he must be gay. But shortly after this instance he was equally unsure yet again. He wasn't into the guys in his school either, which he found irritating. Why was he seeing everyone else experience juvenile blunders at the hands of their presumably natural impulses while he sat idly by and watched? Was there something wrong with him? It was at this time that Steven discovered an article online describing what it was like to live an asexual life. Knowing that other real people felt a general lack of interest in the potential partners around them was supremely reassuring, and for a short period of time he considered himself asexual. For an even shorter period of time he felt content with this attempt.

After Steven completed his high school years, he did start to feel something around confident and experienced older men. He was a strong man himself, however, and it always seemed like these older gay men wanted him subjected to a lifetime of ditzy-gay-boyhood. At one point he handed out a swift but memorable beating to a gay friend for telling him that he needed to choose what he was and not be such an "attention-starved little whore." Steven connected the least with being a whore and also connected little with being belittled, so he decided to be very connected with his knuckles and his accuser's face. A few times.

This event did make Steven question again why he wasn't even able to fit in the LGBTQ spectrum. Perhaps he was bisexual? So he tried dating women for a brief period, to round the whole experience out. Nothing worked. He kind of gave up on the experiment after a while and felt happy with that decision. His feelings of guilt were replaced by a confused absurdity that he did his best to laugh about in the company of his close friends. He was so pleasant and funny and beautiful that he attracted all types. He mixed with women and men, young and old, gay and straight. The only commonality that his friends all possessed was that *none* of them required any type of romantic relationship with him, and that they only wanted his good-natured companionship.

His close friends would meet on Sunday nights in the lounge of a large upscale restaurant that maintained high-level local reviews. That is where he met Chef Josef. Whether he and Josef were going to end up together wasn't even a question to Steven. His friends knew that Josef was gay, and even though Josef didn't understand the interest of a gorgeous man in an obscure cook at an average restaurant, he was in no position to argue when Steven began vying for his attention. Josef had the blessing of not being able to be anything but himself, and things clicked between the two oddballs very quickly, with Steven clearly leading the way romantically.

After a few years of being in love and working separately at jobs they despised, the two renegades decided to venture off on their own with the acquisition of Cigarette's. Steven felt that the consequences of investing all of himself in Josef might be similar to that of giving his whole self to a business that could very well land him in jail. He was scared, and he accepted that, and he had never been so happy. He truly couldn't believe how interesting and rewarding his days were as he spent his time working hard and loving hard with a liveliness and intensity that made him feel at home. He was exactly where he needed to be, with the man he wanted to be with. Steven felt a kind of power in understanding the possible negative consequences of his actions, but he carried through with them anyway. He was confident he could achieve what he desired without ruin and intended to continue enjoying the rewards for years to come.

***

Steven and Josef's relationship enjoyed more success than Cigarette's did in its early stages, and it was reaffirming that they were able to work through the various challenges that they faced and still get along personally. There were *many* challenges to starting a restaurant—especially one with the name Cigarette's during the collapse of the small business food industry, one that was housed in a weird building with a weird past and owned by weird people. They were often risking their freedom when they broke the law, and that had a way of tightening the cuffs of their commitment. They needed to constantly be thoughtful of their efforts. It was exhilarating.

Even though Josef managed to make it sound like buying a bell pepper was on the same plane as obtaining nuclear arms, the reality was that anyone could purchase spices from any supermarket and anyone could create any type of sauce he or she desired at home; just not for sale. The prices for these types of ingredients, however, were, as Josef would reiterate, "too damn high." Initially, when demand had gone down for fresh produce, prices had dropped. But after factories and trade routes had closed up and importing had become more costly and more difficult, prices reflected these changes. Josef could cook anything he wanted for himself, legally, but anything he wished to serve the public required prepackaging and FDA approval, and that became his primary roadblock to creation.

The cost for these preapproved ingredients was kept low as a way to pacify small businesses with "the greatest opportunity in history for the food and beverage industry to turn profits." This kind of rhetoric was such an insult to the owners of recently closed businesses that the intensity of the propaganda directly correlated with the number of local suicides. The preapproved products available for sale were all predictable, bland, and way over-preserved. Also, the rules governing disposal, usage, preservation, and expiration dates were extremely strict and led to an abundance of waste. As consumerism and chemical food production boomed, not only small restaurants but also their suppliers and servicing industries peeled off dead, altogether like a snake shedding its skin.

Every time he and Josef ate out, Steven saw the problems as opportunities shining in front of him. They were constantly underwhelmed during his and Josef's dinner dates. Before the new regulations, eating at different small restaurants was an important and enjoyable ritual. It presented an adventure and the enjoyment of experiential conversation. However, there was no longer any fun in going out, and Steven knew there was a huge number of disappointed people missing the same outlet. A restaurant that broke the law, satisfied customer desires for great food, with owners smart enough not to get caught, was the dream.

Finally, after yet another bland meal at a horribly depressing mom-and-pop place that likely had only a few months left before shutting its doors, Steven had had enough. They were walking back home and when Steven glanced over, Josef had a blank uninvolved kind of contentment on his face, like a weathered statue. He strode along with his left arm wrapped lazily around Steven's waist. Steven looked down at the pavement as they walked, scowling at the pebbly, deteriorating concrete.

"Let's start an eatery, Joe," he blurted out, still watching the pavement lines and cracks pass slowly under his plodding footsteps.

Josef laughed out loud. Hard. Steven knew that he wasn't intentionally mocking him, but he was still a bit offended by the natural response to something that sounded completely absurd. Steven scowled and continued.

"I'm fully serious this time. We need to make a move, and this is the only direction that would let us grow and be the best versions of ourselves."

"You have got to be kidding…" Josef said, squeezing Steven's shoulder. "I would never be able to take pride in my work in this type of environment, Steve. I could never really cook anything that would show what I'm capable of without getting closed down or thrown in jail."

Steven kept his head firmly bowed. He could tell that Josef would rather move the conversation elsewhere, but he was too irritated to give up yet.

"But you do take pride in your work! You serve the best food you can anywhere you are and you always have. Your musings about helping others get more pleasure out of the mundane was one of the many reasons I fell in love with you ... along with all your craziness."

"That's true, but right now I work under someone else's title. The place I work at now may serve slightly better crap than the other places around it, because of me, but it is *exactly that*. It's *crap*. My restaurant..."

"Our restaurant," retorted Steven, without missing a beat.

"Right, *our* restaurant would represent *us* as individuals and leave the mark of our existence. If my creativity is confined against my will during my lifetime, then this is an era that doesn't deserve my mark. May my current presence fizzle out and be reborn into something else with more potential."

"If you're reincarnated you better find me again," Steven said sternly.

"I'll just keep killing myself until I do," Josef replied quickly.

"Aw, you're sweet." Steven finally broke his tough guy attitude and smiled a bit.

Josef's somewhat goofy smile stared back at him warming his spirit.

"I'm not suggesting we follow the rules," Steven said, getting back to his point. "We just appear to follow the rules and pump out the best food we can create, illegally I suppose, but smartly enough not to get caught. It would have to be a mix of using the ingredients demanded of us and our own recipes."

"What if we get caught?" Josef asked.

"Then we fail! Screw it! Then we will move again to some other place and both do exactly as we are told, again. But we have to take a chance. We know a lot of people around here, and they would be excited to try our food. Then we can slowly up the taste ante for our more trusted customers until they understand what we are doing and want it too damn much to care."

"This is a crazy plan, so I am certainly into it at this point," Josef said, finally considering the idea.

"You know?" Steven said rhetorically, agreeing with himself. "It will be this great exercise of our wit not to get caught. We will have to think everything out and work harder than we've ever worked before. But it will be *ours*."

"Ha! And we would get to be bad little boys every damn day." Josef ground his teeth together lightly in anticipation.

"Bad boys were always my favorite," Steven said, trying to mix the perfect amount of viciousness and playfulness together in his words.

"You are selling this very well, Steven, and it's insanely attractive," Josef said.

Steven was pleased with being seen as an object of desire. Josef reinforcing his sense of rebellion made his muscles tighten a bit, and for the moment he felt like he had always held such power. "I sell everything well. It's strange, but that's what I was damn well born to do. I'm a terrific waiter and I am proud to be one."

His making a living serving tables always seemed strange to his friends, because they were used to seeing people who looked like him being served and not the other way around. Serving didn't just come naturally to Steven—it was as if he was put on earth to bring sustenance, warmth, and pleasure to others. He liked being on his feet, he liked keeping things organized and clean, he liked the smell of food, but more than anything he loved people. Especially the odd and out of place ones.

Josef wasn't about to be undone by Steven's enthusiasm. "And I'm the best chef either of us has ever dreamed of, so if we fail we'll get drunk and burn the place down with us inside of it, so no one else can experience our magic here ever again." He finished his thought with a big smile and a confident nod.

Steven laughed and shook his head. "Wow … Josef …

Slow it down a bit, hey?" As usual he was pleasantly shocked by

Josef's ramblings, and as usual he wasn't really surprised.

***

Josef was somewhat melodramatic, even though he was a bear in

the gay community. Graying, impenetrable stubble covered his

face. His eyebrows, although a little overworked, were still burly as

caterpillars, which made his vivid green irises look exceptionally

intense. His long eyelashes gave him an appealing exotic look that

upon further inspection softened this effect quite well. His small

protruding gut looked strong like an ape's, and the full effect of his

presence had an intimidating aura contrary to his actual kind and

sensitive nature.

Josef was far from aggressive, but it was agreed that

handling people would be left up to Steven, who possessed more

socially passable conversation skills. From the time the customers

113

got through the door until the time they left, either raving about their favorite spot or complaining about the treatment they received, it was up to Steven to mold them into the type of customers that they wanted around. Josef did enjoy a bit of drama, though, and whether conscious of it or not, if things were going too smoothly he would usually end up doing something to shake Cigarette's up.

A bad web review could potentially hurt their business, but Josef didn't have the capacity to coddle anyone. Only a handful of times had there been any real problems. The situations always stemmed from new customers with presumptuous attitudes looking to manifest their general displeasure with life in a place somewhere outside their own homes. Sometimes Josef would swear in the kitchen, sometimes he would throw things in frustration, and sometimes he would even get caught pouring himself a shot of whiskey at the bar before heading back into the kitchen to do some more prep work. Most customers shared a good-natured laugh, along with Steven, while taking in the show, but some considered his behavior unacceptable. If anyone needed to take up an issue with Cigarette's, Steven would usually be the one left to clean up the mess Josef created.

Cigarette's received zero stars from a customer who'd erupted in disgust after seeing his plate of food thrown in the trash can beside the cash register, right before it was going to be served.

Josef remembered hearing the small, bewildered smack of lips parting as the customer watched his prospective meal go to waste.

"Complimentary tea?" Steven had asked semi-apologetically.

Josef yelled, "I'll be back with a better effort right away. I never know what I find until I throw it away."

The customer said nothing and stormed out. The next day Josef and Steven read the short post online:

"Cigarette's is exactly as disgusting as its name would imply. I thought I would give the restaurant a try as I have never been a judgmental person, and all I ever want is a good honest meal, and I had all of my expectations thrown in my face. It seems like Cigarette's is owned by a couple of drunk perverts, and I'm lucky they were so drunk that they actually threw my food away right in front of my eyes before I could try it. I probably would have died if I'd eaten there anyway, which is exactly what that horrible business needs to do: die as soon as possible. Boycott this crap factory. Zero stars."

"Josef, you need to try to take it easy. These reviews are really important," Steven said after reading the backlash, clearly a little upset with being criticized. Josef could tell that this time Steven was more shaken up than usual because the review was mostly warranted.

Josef responded thoughtfully while unloading hot dishes from the dishwasher. "The only thing that's important is to be easy every day. Be easy and important, and everything will fall into place. Not everyone will take what we give, but we just need to keep giving what we have."

Steven sighed heavily still tapping away at the tablet, presumably writing a response to the review.

Josef could be a thought-provoking individual even if the images a listener conjured in their imagination in no way matched the point Josef was trying to convey. To reach his point, which usually came with merit, he needed to brazenly smash through the confines of language, and the effect for the listener of Josef's unorthodox speech was a catalyst for thought. His jokes weren't often overly funny, even to himself, but he had to utter them regardless. The effort to subvert the trials of daily life with humor was usually appreciated by Steven but today they seemed to be falling short.

Even with Steven ignoring him Josef still didn't questioned his own ramblings. He always moved on from one idea to the next quickly. The only things that remained stationary in his life were his love for Steven and his love for cooking and he felt certain that nothing he said could change that. He also loved his dog, Cerberus, and his restaurant, Cigarette's, but he understood that these things could be taken away and he would still manage to move on. Alternatively, he would rather die than lose his ability to cook or the blessing of being with his beloved Steven.

Steven set the tablet down on counter and took a deep breath.

"Alright, Joe. Just be careful. We are finally making enough money to continue operating from month to month. Hell, if we can maintain this marginal success, perhaps we can even do this from year to year."

For once Josef conceded. "Yeah, alright Steve. We're actually getting okay, and I hope that we can stay okay because it feels pretty great."

Josef continued putting the dishes away without thinking much about what he said and began washing up to get ready to cook. Steven pulled a trash bag out of its can and paused for a second before carrying it en route to the back door.

Josef heard him say under his breath, "Wow. Okay really does feel good..."

Josef smiled and began chopping an onion. He heard Steven grunt to lift up the reinforced garbage bag into the huge bin outside. A tinge of guilt squirmed into his chest for making such a pretty man do such grunt work but Josef would never have been able to lift that much weight. The bag was brimming with partially used boxes of powder and cans/jars half full of various liquids.

It would have looked far too suspicious not to use any of the pre-approved ingredients so Josef bought the better of what was available and made sure he had just enough on hand of anything else required to make a new customer a fairly predictable meal. He would make sure that each part of the meal was perfectly cooked and that it was put together as beautifully as possible but this was essentially the limit of his capabilities in that scenario. For his regulars though, he may use a bit of the pre-approved stuff for the base but by the end of his preparation the dish would be unlike anything else available. Perhaps in the whole country. All of the heavy waste was the unavoidable byproduct of Josef's extraordinary gift.

The only other option restaurants had was to get their components rendered and approved in bulk and then packaged in an approved facility to be reopened prior to each meal served. This process grew longer every year and was created for restaurant owners with extremely deep pockets. The result was therefore only available to the elite and was still average at best. Josef wished he could sue every place that had a billboard advertising "Real fresh food!" showing people partying in unattainable bliss. But no one could win a case against them for false advertising, since *fresh* was a relative word, and pulling prepackaged slop out of containers right before a meal was as close to fresh as anyone could expect outside of their own kitchen these days.

Josef turned on two burners, adding butter into one and olive oil to the other. A few dashes of spices and a few squirts of various sauces were placed into each and he could already smell the magic. He thought that whoever came up with the idea of monetizing the desire for unprocessed foods was a masochistic genius. Few other legal restaurants still tried to push through their outrage and add seasoning, but the regulations allowed this only to be in the fresh or dried form, and the addition was only permitted in front of a seated customer. You could still get government-approved ground pepper, ground Parmesan, etcetera, etcetera, but was it really worth going out and paying to receive these basics? Apparently the answer to this question was yes. Yes, people got too lazy or tired or lacked the basic knowledge it required to prepare their own meals. But the experience and pleasure of eating something so perfect that you could neither have dreamed of doing it yourself, nor googled it, was dead.

Josef had closely watched the process of loss over the years. There had been increases in a few various niche businesses. The obvious ones were the growers of basic genetically modified produce that was reduced to pulp and added to as many products as possible that wished to promote the idea of healthy eating. Robotics manufacturers and engineers were also doing quite well finding efficient ways of eliminating human beings from the process of obtaining food and getting it into people's mouths. Salt had also never held such a high market value. There were so many varieties of flavored salt that any home without at least half a dozen different kinds would have seemed strange to any thirsty guest.

All drinking water that any civilized person would consider ingesting came from bottles, and most affordable bottled water came from the huge desalinization plants dotted along the coastlines. The removed salt was blended with cheap peppers and oregano (and more often than not, artificial laboratory flavors) and then sold for more than a thousand percent markup.

Without much year-to-year Arctic ice to speak of, Josef remembered being surprised that the oceans hadn't risen even higher than the current flooding problems. Entire coastal cities should have very well been wiped out. He thought that perhaps the answer to this remainder lay within the swelling water factories and his own species' massive bloated populations. Josef imagined that if every person on the planet died and dried up at once, the resulting storms would break every dike on the planet and wash all of the shriveled corpses out to the recovering sea. The thought made him smile.

He was startled when he heard Steven pipe up behind him.

"Our favorite couple of drunks just walked in." Steven said as he passed by Josef with two frosted pint glasses.

"Ah, Kalvin and Jesse." Josef replied excitedly. "Perfect! We could use some excitement around here, I have a feeling we are going to be supremely busy tonight."

"Be careful what you wish for my dear," Steven replied. Josef watched Steven expertly filling the two drafts, their foam building to the top, threatening to spill over the sides.

"Try to get some food orders out of them before they get too sloppy." Josef requested.

"Of course," Steven replied as he rounded the corner. "You just make sure you don't throw out any meals tonight. Do you think you can handle that?"

With Steven out of sight Josef turned back to his pans and stared straight ahead coldly. He seized one of the handles and tossed about the contents over the heat.

"I can do that."

A bit of the sizzling butter popped out and landed on his arm. Josef didn't flinch.

"I can do anything."

Chapter 9, Experiments

Beads and snakes of silty water sat on the whitish-plastic, oval-shaped tables in the smoking pit outside the side door of Cigarette's. The clouds had recently parted, revealing sporadic patches of blue that carried warmth from the cosmos when the holes aligned themselves between the two smokers enjoying the outdoors and the young sun above them. Jesse and Kalvin always sat at the table farthest from the door so that they could pet and play with Cerberus while having a smoke. The simultaneous charity and pleasure made them feel a little bit like kings. Jesse looked across the table and saw his friend Kalvin taking off his fitted leather jacket. He must have been getting too hot, so he removed it from his arms, leaving it to hang over his slouching shoulders and the back of his chair.

The jacket and a pair of massive unadorned black sunglasses covered most of Kalvin's skin whenever he was outside. The sun shone, right then, on his pale arms, emphasizing some sporadic albeit artistically rendered tattoo work. His right arm was lean and strong-looking. His left arm, however, was a functional wreck. A piece of his forearm muscle and a portion of tattoo had been replaced by a band of reddish scar tissue that looked like a tongue. It still made Jesse a bit squeamish when he looked at it. There were two thick crescent-shaped scars running from Kalvin's elbow to his wrist on his right arm, and the portion of his bicep that was showing suggested a further mess under his clean white shirt.

Jesse stared at Kalvin's conspicuous appendage before averting his eyes when Kalvin looked up after lighting his smoke. Jesse pretended to be looking past Kalvin's tarnished body at Cerberus the dog, whose muzzle was pointed up at the sky while Kalvin scratched behind both ears. Cerberus arched his neck up, coaxing the familiar fingers deeper into the soft folds of his skin.

"Clip Cerberus to his run, and let him move around a bit," Jesse said with a little upward head movement that indicated *over there.* Kalvin nodded an acknowledgment and leaned back, taking another drag on his smoke. His jeans were a little wet from the moisture that had remained on his chair even after he had dumped off the pool of water before sitting down. He brushed at his wet shirt and pants a bit as he got up to unclip Cerberus from his current leash. The short leash was for Cerberus to stay close to Cigarette's when no one was watching him. It was also positioned so that he could only reach one of the two plastic tables outside, in case anyone wanted a little extra distance from the pooch. All the regulars knew the dog to be a gentle, harmless creature who seemed eerily intelligent due to his immediate obedience. Alternatively, newcomers were frightened by the muscular-looking shepherd-boxer-cross.

At one time, after a stern lecture from a group of ladies, one of whom had been frightened by the wet nose of the friendly dog attempting to nudge some attention his way, Josef decided to create some distance between man and beast. He cleaned and rearranged the tables and moved one table closer to the back door, which was farther away from Cerberus. He assumed convenience would outweigh conflict, and he was usually correct in this assumption.

When Kalvin approached Cerberus to put him on the longer leash, Cerberus got up quickly. He rocked his weight forward to his powerful front leg and then, with a quick sideways jump, his back legs propped him up and his tongue hung out his mouth with some slow, excited panting. Without Kalvin saying a word, Cerberus hopped over to the post nearby, which he knew to be his play area. Kalvin found the clip end of a long leash that Josef had constructed. Cerberus hopped a little closer to Kalvin's hand, and his large ironically studded collar was clipped to the leash. Kalvin scratched his buddy under the chin.

"Good dog, Cerb, good dog," he said sincerely. "Go have some fun, partner."

The two young men looked out over the trash-littered weeds in the neighboring lot and watched the dog trotting about, sniffing at the debris as a small group of laughing kids roamed nearby. Kalvin took a deep haul on his factory cigarette, nearly smoking into the golden filter. He let out a deliberate huff of smoke and hovered the tiny bright coal over a tin full of gravelly sand and other cigarette butts.

When patrons of Cigarette's would play with Cerberus or watch him play in the dog run in the neighboring yard, he would take full advantage of the attention. Kalvin chuckled as Cerberus grabbed a piece of rope and, while play-growling, shook it back and forth, instinctively killing the flaccid object. Cerberus stumbled a bit while trying to stretch one end of rope between his teeth and the pointed end held by his front paw. Jesse thought about how the dog was attempting to tear apart the flesh of the toy for sport. He looked so happy and fulfilled. It was what he was born to do.

"Don't you think naming a three-legged dog after a three-headed monster is kind of an asshole thing to do?" Jesse commented, breaking what was, to him, an uncomfortable silence.

"What? Cerberus is a perfect name. It sounds perfect," Kalvin replied.

"Maybe. It just seems kind of mean and unnecessary to highlight his handicap."

Jesse could see Kalvin thinking and digging around in the pockets of his jacket for something. "That's nonsense, he *deserves* a name that carries respect."

Jesse still wasn't finished with his disapproval. "The dog might not know the significance of his name, but I believe that animals are fairly tuned into people's emotions, and he can certainly understand that people are laughing at his misfortune." Jesse scratched the stubble on his chin. "And, since he is a product of the way people treat him, maybe a better name would have served him better."

Kalvin snickered. "I sort of agree with you."

Jesse was surprised that Kalvin had changed his opinion so rapidly and was curious as to why, "What do you mean?"

Kalvin tapped the unlit end of his smoke on the table. "Well, I agree that the dog is a product of his environment. But look at how badass and great he is?" Kalvin called out Cerberus's name loud enough to break the dog's concentration at his current game. "Cerberus!" he shouted.

Cerberus dropped his toy and looked toward the source of the sound of his name with his nearly useless eyes wide open and with his spectacular ears tuned directly to Kalvin, completely ready for whatever might happen next.

"You're a *good dog,* Cerberus, *good boy!*" Kalvin said excitedly.

Cerberus wagged his tail and let his tongue loll freely again. His posture relaxed, and after a few seconds he went back, kicked at the bit of rope on the ground with his one front paw, and reanimated his game of kill once again.

"There you have it bro, it looks to me like he is pretty happy with his name. And maybe we all shouldn't take ourselves so bloody seriously, hey?" Kalvin posed to Jesse.

Jesse was a bit embarrassed but couldn't help but agree.

Kalvin let his Cigarette hang loosely from his lips. He took a quick puff before propping the burning white rod up against a rock someone had inexplicably left on the table. Jesse watched him as he reached down into the neat folds of his sock and pulled out two capsules. He quickly swallowed them after a sharp smack of his hand to his mouth and a snap of his head backward in a repeated jerking motion.

Jesse had seen the pills gulped down dozens of times before. He was annoyed. "What the hell, Kalvin?" Jesse said. "You need to drop that shit or I'm going to end up a sad, angry, friendless bastard one day soon, and I'll never forgive you for that."

Kalvin was not amused. "Are you serious? Right now, are you being serious?" Kalvin hissed and squinted his eyes at his opponent. He didn't wait for an answer. "There are people who have spent reasonably pleasant lifetimes on basically the same meds as these. The only difference is I'm lucky enough to actually enjoy them and smart enough to avoid some of the nasty consequences by controlling my dosage and mixing everything right. It's very basic biochemistry, my friend. Read a fucking book someday."

Jesse loved Kalvin, but often he couldn't imagine any other person being nearly as stupid or as frustrating. The feeling was mutual.

"Don't patronize me, dickhead, you're no doctor. And 'mixing everything right' by using a set of measuring spoons is some childish, bullshit nonsense."

Jesse knew Kalvin's drug use intimately. Kalvin enjoyed talking about drugs and reliving his highs and even the foulness of his lows, but he loathed talking about these experiences as "a problem." Jesse cared about his friend enough that he didn't give a damn about what he did or did not wish to discuss.

Kalvin looked uncomfortable and moved around on his seat. "Me not being a doctor is a technicality," he said. "I have a few *other* friends who are pretty sharp in this respect, and although they don't always agree with what I'm doing, they always keep me straight in terms of mixing and amounts." Jesse knew some of these same individuals and didn't buy this logic but allowed Kalvin to continue. "The liver is hardier than we give it credit for if you drink lots of water and eat healthy." This was true-ish. "And what? I'm supposed to listen to you? You burn more dirty ditch weed than any hippie I know and pollute your lungs from that shit that hardly even does anything for you. Except blows your memory." This was gospel.

Kalvin's defensiveness when confronted was a knee-jerk reaction. Jesse felt that Kalvin was too old to be still so affixed to the rebellious image of his youth. It seemed like he linked a feeling of adulthood to substance abuse, but Jesse saw it as more of a showcase of his immaturity.

Jesse literally rolled his eyes at the dig at his marijuana smoking. "Hey, at least I'm actually supporting real enterprising dudes like us, while you're just a pill-popping cog in the system."

"The *system*?" Kalvin laughed out loud and grinned. "Listen to yourself hippie."

Jesse kept rolling, unfazed. "The pharmaceutical corporations know that there are thousands and thousands of people just like you absorbing the surplus of their bloody mystery powders." Jesse paused briefly with his mouth still open. "You. Support pharmaceutical companies. For shit's sakes." Jesse shot his judgments at Kalvin in short blasts. "They have been the devil for eons."

"You don't think the government controls your goofy pot-smoking minions?" Kalvin threw back.

"Absolutely not."

"Yeah, you're probably on the good side of that issue," admitted Kalvin. "Listen though, Jesse, as righteous as you know that I know that you know that I *know* I am, I just can't care about the industry in this, the one millionth of a percentile, in which I choose to ingest."

Jesse grabbed Kalvin's pack of cigarettes and bummed one without asking. Jesse usually didn't smoke, and even though he may have won the debate, he felt like sometimes Kalvin let him have the victory in order to change the subject. Kalvin always teeter-tottered any arguments he was losing by suddenly becoming self-righteously passive. Jesse was frustrated by this technical maneuver in futility, and instead of wasting more of his time he decided to stick a cigarette in the way of his words.

After a few minutes of silent smoking and staring, Kalvin piped up. He had his elbow on the table and his fist bobbed gingerly in front of his face. He used the outstretched thumb and forefinger occasionally to emphasize a point. Kalvin's rambling became more animated as the desired high kicked in.

"It's all about energy..." he began, which seemed to Jesse to be out of nowhere. "And not that metaphysical bullshit that you hippies talk about three minutes after hitting the bong every time. No offense."

Jesse snickered in spite of himself. "None taken."

"I'm talking about expending calories, readied muscles, and a sharp understanding. Awareness..."

Jesse had no clue where this was going, but he settled in and continued to puff on his cigarette a little awkwardly.

Kalvin continued. "Our basic biomechanics are operating as they're meant to. You need to focus in order to live and function properly or you're just a slug. Take a minute sometime and watch worms that have been forced out of the earth after a heavy rain. They just fucking lie there, barely moving. That's *exactly* what I see every time I look out into the streets. People dragging their heels around, *slogging* from one place they feel they are supposed to be to the next one. Wasting their potential, living blind, deaf, sexless, while their insides are on the edge of action just waiting for the right nudge to go fucking crazy, pumping at their capacity, running for their damned lives!" Kalvin stopped for a second to put his pack of cigarettes back in his jacket.

"So drugs are your *little nudge* to live your life to its fullest?" Jesse said, in disbelief at what he was hearing. "What if you're really just peaking and ebbing all the time, and the culmination of that is really less than you could make if your brain was working more smoothly. What if you could make more methodical moves instead of just racing around hoping that you're moving more forward than back?"

"Tried that," Kalvin said through a puff of smoke.

"Yeah, *everyone* thinks they tried that, since at one time *everyone* was a child, and they were sober then. Shit. I'm talking about being a sober, balanced adult with experience and settled hormones."

"You're one to talk! You're damn near outer space high every night," Kalvin said.

"You can kiss my hippie ass," Jesse said.

"Well, I know that you're talking about being a sober adult, Jesse. Christ. And I'm saying that I have tried *that.* I woke up tired, went to work tired, worked tired, and came home… really fucking tired! Tell me what the hell is the point of living like that? Living longer? But I don't *enjoy* living like that. Why, then, would I want to do something I don't *enjoy* even longer?"

This was a universal truth that not only did Kalvin and Jesse agree on but was one of the pillars of their relationship.

Jesse still felt Kalvin was headed in the wrong direction, though, and tried to sway him. "Maybe the point is to get to a place that you do enjoy, even if it's hard at first, after which you can squeeze as much joy as possible from the path you choose to take?" All the while, suggesting the satisfaction he attempted to cultivate through his own lifestyle.

"Oh, bullshit," Kalvin scoffed.

"Yeah?" challenged Jesse, pointing with both of his index fingers at two rows of straight white smiling teeth. Kalvin had his arms already crossed and had been leaning on them increasingly during the conversation.

"Bullshit," Kalvin repeated. "We've been in a recession that's lasted a hundred fucking years. The powers that be want us to live like this, Jesse—dumbed down and happy to barely get by. Then we die from some disease that we had nothing to do with creating, while never having had the intelligence to enjoy the ride."

"Whatever, I'm enjoying my ride and I don't have to be bumped out of my mind all the time," posed Jesse.

"Trust me, you're not enjoying it as much as I am right now," said Kalvin, while pretending to flail around out of control.

Both men laughed and relaxed a bit. Cerberus met their gaze while lying on the ground at the end of the yard. His leash was tight enough that it pulled his collar away from his neck on the side of his head closest to submission. His toy, the piece of rope, hung satisfactorily limp on his front paw. He panted rapidly. He let his tongue drop out the front of his mouth as far as it wanted to go, and his eyes were only half open as he lay in the dirt in bliss.

Chapter 10, the Dog

Cerberus would have made a good person. He was able to approach every new day with excitement, he was a showcase of contentment, he listened a great deal more than he spoke, and he gave and received affection lovingly. Unlike so many humans who stay so detached from others while remaining unhappily married to their ideas, Cerberus accepted things for what they really were and, save for some types of violent adversity, this allowed him to thrive throughout his life. His poor black-and-white vision allowed his other senses to perceive the deeper and truer beauty of his surroundings and its inhabitants. A human's vision often complicates things and can lie to even the keenest rationalist.

Cerberus took what he could get whenever he got it, including affection, toys, treats, and walks. He would have been fine with standard dog food, but the food that he was served was exceptional. Josef would sort through the variety of leftovers and raw scraps and would take his time determining what would be healthy for Cerberus. This was nice, but food was exceptional for Cerberus, just because it was edible and available. He would wolf down anything put in front of him, except peas. After noticing how Cerberus left behind peas anytime they were in his dish, Josef once counted out the peas he put into some leftover stew he gave to Cerb for breakfast. He was stupefied to find each one unscathed in the bottom of Cerberus's bowl that was otherwise licked clean. If the dog did have standards, they were uncompromising, albeit few.

Any of the regulars at Cigarette's would know where to find Cerberus. He would either be running himself into exhaustion playing on his long leash, or he would be resting deeply on his plush and hairy brown mat near the rear entrance, chewing on a toy or a bone. Either of these activities could be dismissed immediately if someone wanted to interact with him, though. He leaned into people's offerings of scratches and pats so hard that he had toppled a few small children and the occasional drunk.

Sometimes he would even lean hard enough to fall on his own face if someone moved away too quickly. The people always felt sorry for the lovable three-legged dog when they saw his missteps, but his falls were more the effect of Cerberus's overzealousness than the results of his disability.

He would close his eyes whenever he felt another's affection laid on him. He would lose himself completely to their generosity and the pleasure it brought. At those moments, nothing existed outside this pleasure. A swirling mix of his senses, the physical touch, the slow motion awareness of his environment, the smell of his life, all blended into a sweet murmur of what was once an overwhelming cacophony. When the fun was over though, he once again remained alert enough to notice a blink. The distractions would vanish, and his senses would become more acute. At such times, dangers were more real once again, climates were more extreme, and more than anything, hunger was more pressing.

***

Steven had always run the playlists in Cigarette's that flowed throughout the entire day. During Josef's prep work in the morning, he started things slowly, and the pace increased around the lunchtime mini-rush. Then they had lively music for the few stragglers popping in for coffees, late lunches, and early drinks in the afternoon. Finally, by evening, the music consisted of relaxed remixes of current hits and old favorites. At the end of the day, during cleanup, Steven would toggle between a few of his favorite Internet radio stations or listen to a podcast about a topic that he was interested in.

When Josef and Steven had to leave Cerberus alone, they would leave the music playing so that he would think they were right around the corner. One day, Josef and Steven had to visit the doctor's office. They gave Cerberus some affection and said they would be right back. Unfortunately, they were in a rush and forgot to push Play as they struggled to make the appointment. It didn't take much more than two hours for the doctor to prescribe some antibacterial and anti-inflammatory cream for Josef's sore shoulder stump. As they walked back together, Josef thanked Steven for dragging him out of his stubbornness to seek relief. As soon as they opened the door from this pleasant journey, they saw the mess Cerberus had created in their absence.

He had pissed on the floor what looked like several times, he had torn many of their bench cushions to shreds, and he had ripped apart their cleaning supplies: brushes, brooms, mops, buckets, and toilet paper. Thankfully, they had kept all of the chemicals on shelves or among the mess would have also been a dead dog. Instead, the young pup was shaking and cowering in the closet where he usually slept. Although both Steven and Josef were furious at first, since they had never seen Cerberus act in any way like this, they didn't yell at him or beat him. They both leaned into the closet and coaxed the fear out of the broken pup and then led him outside to relax in the warm, cloudy afternoon while they cleaned up.

After Cerberus had torn apart Cigarette's, Josef and Steven were still able to go out together as long as they left music playing. This was the last mess that Cerberus ever made, aside from his daily dumps in the vacant lot outside. The consistency of these deposits was entirely based on the dog's diet, which Josef controlled with scientific precision. Josef and Steven took turns cleaning up the dog's waste, and neither of them really minded the job. A few good, firm poops every day were mutually beneficial for man and beast. Cerberus did still have "pee accidents" when he was frightened, but usually thunder was the culprit, and that was occasional enough not to be a real bother.

This incontinence was all caused by fear. Cerberus had not been alone, locked behind a man's door in a quiet space, since Josef had discovered him nearly two years earlier in an abandoned building. The quiet evoked as much fear as the roar of atmospheric charges colliding. Raucous sounds and noiselessness terrified Cerberus, but it was the gentlest whimper that had saved his life. Josef thanked God that he had heard the cries in the abandoned building that day. In fact, he prayed then, for the first time since his childhood. He had been in the right place at the right time. He was so thankful for being there, however he had gotten there, just that one crucial time.

At daybreak, two years earlier, Josef had been smoking outside on the patio, sipping a cup of black coffee. Just as he got up to go inside he heard a whining in the normally quiet early morning hours. He crept toward the sound, which was coming from the boarded-up building across the empty lot behind Cigarette's. If it hadn't been early morning, the possibility of inhabitants may have kept him away. It sounded to him like a dog might have been trapped within the decaying building's guts. Josef had always liked dogs and decided that he had enough time to investigate.

The plywood on the front door had been mostly pried off and clung on by only a few bent nails, making it easy enough for anyone or anything to gain access or egress. Once inside, he quietly made his way up a set of stairs as the whimper grew a fraction louder in the vacuum. As he crested the stairs, he saw a scene that nothing in his life could have prepared him for. Blood, rope, and several hypodermic needles were scattered around the floor. At one end of the room, there was a man seemingly passed out on a torn and filthy mattress, and at the other end there was a dog tied to the base of a chair, whining weakly and missing one of his front legs. Josef looked back and forth a few times in disbelief. He realized that what remained of the dog's missing leg was actually lying at the base of the mattress in front of the man, and that there were definite signs that he had been recently … eating it. Josef actually covered his mouth, which had been unknowingly hanging open, in horror. He had never been a confrontational man, but he was certainly more substantial than the addict who had yet to even move, and regardless of size Josef's adrenaline was flowing through him in a way he had never felt before. The fury he felt was physically enabling but was also disabling in the sense of his usual good judgment.

He grabbed a board off the floor immediately and whacked the man on the bare mattress, who groaned and moved only a little. He considered whacking him again, but harder. Instead he dropped the board and focused his attention on the dog. He decided the best thing to do was take the remainder of the rope used to tie up the dog and incapacitate the already unmoving man. This was done fairly easily, almost like tying back the legs of a turkey, and in much the same manner. The man was more or less a limp bag of lifeless meat. The man threw up a bit when he was rolled on his side and he groaned and flinched more or less involuntarily. *Perhaps he's in the early stages of an overdose,* Josef thought. *I should have left him to choke on his dog-meat vomit.*

Following this, he untied the injured dog, who didn't resist and in fact licked Josef's arm, even though he couldn't feel it. Josef glanced back at the bound man and, satisfied that he would remain bound, he ran down the stairs and back to Cigarette's, holding firmly to the dog in his arm, and whispering *"Shhh, shhh"* in an attempt to soothe his whimpering. The dog must have also been sedated, because he seemed barely conscious and was not exhibiting pain like Josef would have expected. Perhaps the psychopath had been using the same drugs on both man and animal.

"Call a veterinarian!" Josef screamed at Steven when he got inside Cigarette's.

"A veterinarian? What? What the—?" Steven stammered in confusion.

"Just get a fucking veterinarian for this dog!" Josef yelled again, this time with tears coming down his face, unable to control himself.

"I, I don't know anyone … Josef, I'm going to call … Oh, wait! I know a Doctor Without Order; I'll call Cynthia up and she can help!"

Steven quickly found the phone number on the screen of his phone and made a call. Josef never demanded anything of Steven, making the presence of actual demands seem unquestionably urgent. He sat down and began petting the dog with his good arm and holding it close in his lap. The dog's eyes were only partially open, and it looked as if it could drift to sleep, or die.

Steven's phone call was answered. "Yeah, hi, it's Steven from Cigarette's …Yeah … Hey, I need you to get over here right away. I have someone who I think has had an overdose and is missing a leg … Yes. Yes, we have it in a tourniquet … No … I don't know how he lost it … No … Just get over here!" Then he hung up.

Cynthia arrived around fifteen very long minutes later, and after a very brief evaluation she injected the dog with a narcotic antagonist. She clearly wasn't pleased at risking her freedom for veterinarian purposes, but after Josef quickly told her what had happened she obliged. It wasn't long before she had packed her things and given Steven some painkillers to mix into the dog's food and some antiseptic for the leg wound.

She looked at them both apathetically. "Look, the wound shouldn't become infected if you clean it diligently. However it got removed was nothing short of surgery. He's a lucky dog. Oddly, he seems not to be overly traumatized, so you should be able to get close to him. Good luck, you guys, call me only if you need me."

"Thank you very much, Cynthia," Steven said, holding the pup in his arms.

"Yes, thank you," said Josef, his eyes puffy and red.

She stuffed a fistful of cash into her backpack, and as soon as she closed the front door—which had a Closed for Repairs! sign dangling from it, complete with a drawing of a happy looking worker with a hammer—Josef turned to Steven.

"I'm calling William," Josef said firmly, tapping on his phone a few times. "We still have a problem, Steven … William will know what to do. He may be the only man who knows what to do."

***

It was surprising that in only a couple years Cerberus's front leg muscles and tendons had already stretched and repositioned his healthy leg nearly in the center of his body. He seemed much more comfortable at a reasonable run than walking, but overall he got around just fine. The momentum of a run for Cerberus was intoxicating and freeing, yet difficult to come by in the confines of his city life. So he made do with hop-along walks around the city streets, usually with Steven. Often Steven would try to jog a bit to help Cerberus get some rhythm in his stride on their early morning or late night adventures. He cared about socializing Cerb, and about his general well-being, so they rarely missed a day.

Steven had gone to pick up some basic snacks and toiletries from the chipped beige shelves of the local corner store when he saw two different people carrying pet rabbits around. Cerberus had been alerted to the shuffling weirdos carrying the rabbits and was very interested. He didn't lunge or bark at them but did tug harder on the leash, leaning firmly into the delightful smells of potential prey as they passed by. His nose was overwhelmed with the smell of meat and blood beneath the delicate critters' thin skins. Every muscle in his lean body was alight with powerful electric impulses. Steven yanked on the leash a bit and said, "Cerberus. No." Cerberus did his best to calm down.

Recently, pets of all kinds had become noticeably more popular. Domestic foxes and birds of prey had been fairly trendy for the last few years. Stranger still was the greater number of meats being more commonly consumed. Hippo meat had even been finding its way to American shelves somehow. Steven presumed that they were growing genetically modified super hippos in some massive secret underground swamp somewhere. He was sure that was a satisfactory enough answer, anyways.

One guy with his rabbit had on a robin-hood-green felt hat and the other person's pale lower stomach flesh hung out the bottom of his thin T-shirt and flopped over his sparkling yellow pants. Both people seemed equally ridiculous to Steven. He had on his usual fitted jean jacket and worn yet stylish jeans and clean basic white T-shirt. He was a practical purchaser but constantly striving to look sharp with his current favorite pieces. He talked to Cerberus about the bunny-lovers' choices in clothing and pets.

"They must have gotten every one of the ideas they have ever had from a flashing screen. Well, perhaps not the gooey gut hanging out thing ... Wow, is that gross. But the way they dress, the things they buy, the way they carry themselves. It's all presented to them and they submit."

Cerberus looked at the people and then back at Steven and wagged his tail. Steven chuckled. He knew Cerberus didn't understand what he had said, but the dog just loved that Steven was talking to him. He had arrived in their lives by accident but now had a purpose as their companion. Cerberus's beauty was amplified by adversity, and he had fit into Steven and Josef's lifestyle naturally.

When the two goofy bunny fanciers noticed Cerberus they bumbled away wordlessly. Despite Cerberus's tripod predicament he still looked menacing, especially when he was out for a walk and was excited. This was very comforting to Steven, being the fairly slim and handsome young man that he was. Cerberus was never trained to attack and was actually very friendly, and he socialized with all types of beings, both dog and non-dog.

Steven still felt that Cerberus would do *something* if he or Josef were ever in peril, though. He found comfort in this notion. Perhaps Cerberus didn't have an attack mode? In that case, a deterrent was still nice. Regardless, they were a team; each had his role. Steven often thought that he would certainly fight anyone who came after Cerberus. Steven's eyes burned a little and a tear brimmed on one of his lids in the grocery store, but he fought it back and felt a bit silly for getting so introspective and emotional. He smiled, grabbed a few groceries, and he and Cerberus plodded on toward home through the uncertainty and nervousness that came with the fading light.

It was well past dark, and all the customers were long gone when Steven returned. Josef had already cleaned up and was sitting in one of the booths reading and having a snack. Steven came in the front door and walked right over to Josef. He placed

his grocery bags on the floor and some of the items fell on their

sides. A little tin of tea rolled out across the floor, making a light

sandy sound. Steven hugged Josef hard, and Josef's book was

squished for a second between his hairy chest and the top of

Steven's head.

Cerberus crawled under the table and lay down on Josef's

feet, looking up at him and pressing his nose under Josef's hand

and then Steven's hand, essentially petting himself. Steven had

closed many of the emotional doors in his life after every

disappointment, but in this moment he felt childishly exposed. The

basic truths of their lives were stripped down, and their bones

were bleached in the sun of reality. Love. The horribly abused

animal only wanted to be loved and to feel closeness and

companionship. Cerberus pushed his long, soft snout under

Steven's right arm. Steven smiled and scratched hard behind

Cerberus's ears in little circles. He could see the emotions on

Josef's face. His melancholic feelings lived within him but usually under so many layers that they remained unseen. Steven felt like he needed to say something.

"Josef, can you feel your soul in your chest?" He said, smiling and fighting back a waver in his voice.

"I don't know Steve…" Josef replied warily.

Steven didn't wait more than a second to reply. "I can," he said, smiling and resting his head against Josef's. He didn't leave his head there for very long but peered under the table to look at Cerberus's eyes, which were closed gently as he accepted the ear massage. His back leg began to kick rhythmically as Steven kept hitting the spot that apparently took Cerberus to doggy heaven. Steven closed his eyes too and leaned into Josef. He took Josef's prosthetic arm and rested it gently on his leg.

Josef reached across with his good hand and squeezed Steven's thigh, he spoke slowly, and seemed as if he was in a mild trance.

"I know my heart is just a pump with some valves made up of muscle, fat and veins. I have cooked hearts. I have eaten hearts. It doesn't bother me. But your heart injects your soul into your blood, Steve; it nourishes every cell in your body."

"But what about when we die?" Steven asked. He really meant this question—death still scared him a great deal, and spending his afternoon walk thinking about violence had left a heavy weight within him.

Josef shook his head as if to dismiss death and continued on.

"When your cells aren't there anymore, the frequencies your heart made during your life carries on for them, like a phantom. Your soul goes everywhere and echoes who you were. Perhaps into another heart, primarily, or perhaps into several other hearts, or no other hearts at all. But your heart links your mind to your body. Your blood, carrying nutrients and oxygen and your soul, shapes everything." He looked towards Cerberus and hovered his left hand above the dogs head. Steven took this to be him mocking a transcendental power to help soften the heaviness of the moment. The dog was more or less asleep.

"I love you, Josef," Steven said, this time unable to stop the waver in his voice.

"I love you too, Steven," Josef said stoically. He exhaled. "I love you so much."

Chapter 11, Elevation

As a young girl, Anna would explore. All of her free weekend hours were lost to the daylight while she traipsed through the wooded area behind her dirty neighborhood. She was often able to convince a few neighborhood kids to join her on her expeditions, and she enjoyed great success as a tour guide. The little packs of wild children would roam around playing with sticks, rolling rocks down into gullies, or sometimes just sitting in the back of the carcass of an old truck that had been smashed up too far down an embankment to be retrieved. The old truck was the promised climactic summit, after which the kids would turn around and go home with whatever bit of plastic souvenir they chose to rip off. Anna and whichever children had showed up that day would talk for hours in the bed of the immobilized vehicle. They would ask each other questions, laugh at the answers, and pretend that they knew every important thing there was to know.

Of the dozens of times she had visited that truck, one day shone in her eyes like a flashlight through the trees. A larger than usual group had gathered one morning, and by the afternoon they found themselves a long way from the neighborhood. Based on the prodding from some of the older children, they were long past the turning point truck, and although Anna was a little uncomfortable with the decision to venture into the unknown, she began to enjoy the adventure. There was the added comfort of having more, and older, kids present than usual. As they walked further on, she relaxed and noted points of interest for future endeavors.

When they stopped for a break, some of the boys began flipping over logs to look at the strange insects hiding underneath. Anna couldn't believe her good fortune. She had brought a pocket-sized book in her jacket that described dozens of local insects. Seeing little beetles, worms, and pill bugs was fairly standard and she was taking her time inspecting a black beetle with an iridescent stripe on it when someone screamed.

"Eww! What is that ugly thing? Kill it!"

Anna turned to see the "ugly bug" of interest, which happened to be a translucent red centipede. She quickly ran over and placed a log back down on top of the disturbed area.

"That's just a centipede, they like to make their homes under rotten logs," Anna said happily, trying to divert the hatred.

"I don't care what it is," replied the older girl who had screamed earlier. "It's sick, and I'm going to kill it."

"It didn't do anything to you; just leave it alone."

Anna's mom had always told her that every creature had a purpose and that God loved all of his creations, just as she loved Anna.

The older girl was irritated and not interested in backing down. "Listen to me, you little loser, there is nothing you can do to stop me from killing that disgusting thing, so move. Now!"

The girl tried to brush past Anna, but Anna held her ground. She tried again, and Anna sat down on the log. Anna pulled out her book to show the older girl the page with a detailed drawing of a centipede as the other children all stared in silence. She felt scared and angry but stayed seated on the log not knowing what else to do.

"Get the hell out of my way, you stupid Paki!" screamed the girl.

"No!" Anna screamed back.

"Fine," replied the girl. "Screw you and your stupid Paki book!"

Then she tore the book away from Anna with a stiff elbow, hitting her tiny chest and knocking her back. The cruelty did not end there, and the next thing Anna knew she was watching her precious book thrashing through the air as she lay on the ground. The pages flapped violently as it sailed down the hillside toward the river. It hit the dirt partially open and rolled a bit further down the hill before finally hanging up in a bush near the river's edge. Anna's innocent world of kindness came crashing down on her in an avalanche of confusion and painful shock. She got up quickly to look down the side of the bank and could tell that her bug manual was damaged but still retrievable.

Her mouth and her eyes sucked in air, wide open for an instant. Then her intentions turned to tears. She began to bawl, quietly, with her body in spastic tension. She didn't cry often and wasn't sure if she was doing it properly. She felt uncomfortable being watched by the others so without saying a word or even thinking about what she was doing, she began to run down the hill. She needed to get her book back. Her feet slipped out and landed abruptly on her backside and the palms of her hands. This hurt, but she kept going, tasting her first bit of adrenaline. As she slipped and fell several times more, her clothes became covered with brown dirt and bits of moss. Her tears turned into tiny new muddy streams pushing away the debris on her face. The older girl laughed, and a few kids followed the villain over the top of the bank and out of sight. Anna looked back and saw this and finally sat down right where she was and cried hard into her balled-up fists.

To her surprise, a boy her age and two younger girls walked down to the patch of pine-needle-covered moss where Anna had given up.

"It's okay, Anna," the boy said. "We'll get your book back."

The three kids all crawled down the bank, clinging to willow branches and tufts of grass. They formed a little impromptu assembly line, and the boy who went down the farthest retrieved the book, brushed off some of the damp earth, and handed it to the girl above him. This girl unbent a few pages that were folded over and handed it to another girl. The last child crawled up a little higher and handed it to Anna.

"You're not a stupid Paki, Anna. You know all sorts of stuff, and you saved that weird thing. The centipede," the small blonde girl in the oversized jeans said. She was now covered in filth, just like Anna. She looked like she might cry too.

Anna looked at the girl's eyes. She didn't want the younger girl to feel sorry for her or to become upset. She dried off some off her tears with the underside of her sweater and forced a poor attempt at a smile.

"Tha-ank y-you," she said, choking out the sounds. Standing up, she and the younger girl linked arms with the other children as they made their way up the hill. The left-behind foursome took a while to clamber up the hillside, and by the top they all felt like champions. A light, damp happiness hung above them. They walked proudly home, talking about the mean older girl and the other jerks who had left them to fend for themselves.

They all walked to Anna's home together and took excited, emotional turns explaining to her mom what had happened. Anna's mother invited the filthy kids inside for some drinks and cookies. They ate and drank quickly before running home to worried parents. All the children were proud to hold their heads high, even though they were late. Once they had given their respective accounts of heroism, none of them were punished. A child's confidence in the face of wrongful persecution was delightfully persuasive.

It wasn't the cruelty that stuck in Anna's head throughout the years; it was the redemptive kindness of those that were brave enough to help someone standing up for what was right. She swore to herself that she would always wear her kindness on her sleeve and that if she ever needed to take violent action to protect something again, she would do so regardless of the consequences.

***

Anna's eyes tensed into tiny eye-smiles as she recalled the memory of some of her earliest friends. They were probably all still in the same town she had grown up in. It seemed unreachable now, like another planet. She knew she would return to that place again, perhaps even soon, but she would only be able to experience it physically. She had so little connection to the person she once was, or to the person her parents and friends remembered her as. Her heart was here now.

Anna and Aadir had always loved dining out. It was a treat to have someone else prepare their food for them and to discuss the preparation's merit. They stumbled upon Cigarette's simply because it was proximal to where they lived but it didn't take long for them to fall in love it. Perhaps Josef trusted them because of their eccentric clothing. No food inspector would have ever been privy enough or put that much effort into reproducing their getups, and even if he had, Aadir's hair and gangly frame denoted a history of wildness. Whatever the reason, they were served well-spiced burgers, the special that day, and the result was something that took them both back to the happy family dining experiences of their youth. The experience of time travel was something they had never been able to reproduce anywhere else in the city, and although they kept trying new places for fun, they kept going back to Cigarette's again and again.

Initially they felt a little uncomfortable when they visited Cigarette's. The cool glances and reserved conversations that transpired during their first few weeks of patronage were disconcerting. Steven was the only person who was warm and welcoming. In general, they liked to keep to themselves anyway, and the food was so good that they usually had their mouths full. Socializing could wait. Compared to the regular slop houses and fast-food joints that they had tried, it was certainly more expensive albeit tastier, more satisfying, and by all measures healthier.

Over the course of a year Anna and Aadir had become regulars at Cigarette's. Their commitment to the grub had finally earned them some nice social perks as well. They were now greeted by patrons whose names they had learned organically and whose backstories began to emerge. Everyone was so different. The food was so different. It was so enjoyable that they felt the need to pace themselves so that the vibe would last longer.

Anna watched Aadir as his fingers danced rapidly all over the touch-screen table mat in front of him. She could have been browsing the Internet independently, too, but was relaxing and enjoying her coffee instead. She would occasionally peek across at the upside-down version of whatever Aadir was reading, and he had stopped on an opinion piece in a local speak-spot page. These columns were always a toss-up. Usually someone would be communicating their outrage with current local policies and the unfairness that had had a recent negative effect on them. These blogs helped spread awareness of the issues but rarely prompted much afterthought. Sometimes the columns contained someone's loose musing about life, and these were often the real gems, since they were humorous whether the author realized it or not.

The worst prose would leave the reader skimming over semiliterate ramblings in frustration. Anna saw that Aadir had found an opinion piece written by someone who backed up every point with a barely related quote.

"Check this out," he said to Anna. She looked up from sipping her coffee. "'By identifying with our desires and taking them too seriously, we not only increase our susceptibility to disappointment, but we also create a climate inhospitable to the free and easy fulfillment of those desires...' A man named Tom Robbins said this."

Anna rocked her ceramic coffee cup from side to side, taking in the concept.

"I suppose there is some truth to that, considering the general difficulties created by taking things too seriously. People who stress out too much are poor performers." Anna spoke thoughtfully as she stirred her coffee out of boredom.

"I think its crap," Aadir spat out, still looking at the screen. Anna suddenly stopped fiddling with her cup and turned her attention dial up. Aadir looked up at her, grabbed some of his hair to crush in his fingers, and continued.

"I think every person of any real level of influence or success in history or *herstory* has taken his or her pursuits *very* seriously in the sense of drive and willpower. I certainly don't believe this guy was merely referring to not having a sense of humor about things. His sentiment provokes a brief thought, but overall it's a total miss. It misses the point. The point is that every triumph takes sacrifice and dedication, and it certainly isn't free and easy."

Anna considered this for a second, "Maybe he's saying that over exuberance is transparent and detracting and can ultimately lead to difficulties in reaching goals. Maybe he's saying to keep your emotions separate from your pursuits?" She felt pleased with herself. Sometimes she liked to challenge Aadir's ideas more to frustrate him than merely to play devil's advocate. Other times she was unsure of exactly what she really believed in and enjoyed bouncing ideas off him to solidify her own preconceptions, even if this made Aadir's life temporarily more difficult.

"I can appreciate that to some degree, but ... wait." Aadir stopped himself in the midst of a knee-jerk agreement. He continued immediately. "No. Emotions are not just a by-product of experience, they *tell* us things. You taught me that. We must cognize our emotions and use them as a kind of, I don't know, a kind of metaphysical feeler to make better decisions."

"So now you're into the supernatural?" Anna teased.

"I've always been into crazy afterlife and transcendent stuff! Just not so much the institutions that espouse them," Aadir said, a little more on edge than necessary.

"Are you serious, A? We are not going to talk about the church again." Anna had found herself embroiled in religious conversation too often lately.

"Okay … Alright. Let's use us as the example," Aadir replied.

"Okay, let's." Anna was pleased that Aadir was finally summoning the guts to stop steering the conversation away from what he really wanted to talk about.

"I desire you," he said.

"And I appreciate that," replied Anna. Aadir scowled. She could tell that she had hurt his feelings just a bit by not returning his cutesy courtesy.

"Anyways," Aadir continued, "I admit to myself and to you that I love you and want you in my life, as have millions of other people in millions of other situations. To say that by identifying with this we have made the process more arduous is defeatist rambling."

This sounded quite logical. "Hmm," Anna replied slowly. "I guess so."

"You guess that I'm right!" Aadir said, in a comically triumphant fashion.

Anna laughed and sighed at the same time. She took a pull on her cool coffee.

"I guess you're right," she said. "I certainly agree that great accomplishments have been achieved by people who connect strongly with their goals. And I agree that great loves, like ours"— Anna smiled—"are created by people who feel passionately about their relationships and work hard for them … and I will always work hard for you, my love." Anna beamed and looked directly into Aadir's eyes, blocking out everything else in the room. She noticed Aadir's pupils widen slightly as he returned the gesture. She felt like reaching across the table and kissing him but stayed unmoving in their eye lock instead.

"Why don't we head home and put in a bit of that work then?" Aadir said mischievously.

"You are going to make a brown girl blush, my dear," replied Anna, with a dash of humor as she settled back into the booth. She had always thought that good things came to those who were patient. She imagined that if she could keep Aadir patient for the time being, then she could take him home and let him wordlessly rip her clothes off as a reward to them both.

"I'm a lot more talented at working your emotions than you know, my dear," said Anna assertively. She took a big gulp of her coffee and the two lovers were silent for a couple of minutes. Anna was uncomfortable with so much disclosure, she was also a bit aroused. The juxtaposing waves of these feelings surged and finally crashed onto a warm euphoric plane.

Aadir went back to fiddling with the table screen. Anna squinted to read the daily special on a board near the bar. *Heaping Veggie Bastard Lasagna: layers of a parsley–cottage-cheese blend mixed in with grated garlic-butter eggplant, sautéed onion, shredded carrot, and diced celery between folds of pasta covered with jalapeño aged cheddar and mozzarella.* She had watched an anonymous thin man order a piece earlier and had seen his frown turn upside-down as he shoveled the whole plateful clean. The skinny man must have known Steven, because the plain lasagna was taken to the back after a funny little eyebrow raise from the man, and when it was returned hot, the smell was hypnotizing.

Steven came over, smiling gaily as usual.

"You two lovebirds still good with the coffees?"

"No, sir," replied Anna enthusiastically. "We are going to have to have a piece of whatever that is." She pointed to the board.

Steven smiled and snapped his fingers once, pointing to Anna. "You are to make sure you let him have a bit of it as well, hey?"

They all chuckled and Steven turned to yell out the order to Josef, who never replied but always heard.

"Another special Josef. And make it a special special!"

Anna watched Josef take a piece of the standard lasagna from the display tray to the back for its preparatory embellishment. She began to lightly chew on her lip.

"Be just a minute, friends," said Steven. He often referred to his regulars as friends, and they were. It was comforting to hear Steven say the word. It was part of his character, so the term was a bit of an idiosyncrasy, but at the same time he meant it.

Aadir turned back to Anna. "How did you end up turning into such a food lover and expert anyway?" he said, referring to her typical adventurousness and trying to steer the conversation away from anything the least bit sexy.

Aadir tended to patronize Anna without noticing it or without meaning any harm. This was a by-product of what had become a largely womanless life for Aadir. Given the amount of time spent with a very close and intense father early in his life, and then the time needed to take care of a distant father in his more recent adulthood, he questioned everyone and was generally skeptical.

"That sounds like something you city boys would say after spending too much time watching television. Some things are inherent to our nature that you men will never understand, no matter how much you read. Or, in your case, watch on television," she added playfully.

"True. We city boys watch far too much television. But you country girls think we can somehow read what you're thinking. I think TV taught me that too. Not that it has helped much—"

A clamor came from the back of the kitchen.

Chef Josef fumbled a large metal spoon and it came to rest on the ground. "Ass-piss!" he hissed, squinting at the recently dropped item. He leaned over with a low sigh and picked it up. Anna watched him as he quickly glanced through the doorway behind him and tossed the utensil, which clanged victoriously into the sink against the other end of the wall.

Both Anna and Aadir laughed out loud.

"Who says 'ass-piss' in a restaurant?" Aadir asked and then went back to searching through the Internet for something else that piqued his interest.

Anna finished the dregs of her coffee and got up to go have a smoke and pet Cerberus. "I'll be right back," she said as she leaned in for a kiss. She could smell another pile of lasagna being heated up just for them, and she noticed her mouth watering.

Chapter 12, Roadblocks

When Cigarette's opened, it appeared to still require at least another month of work to be fit for public scrutiny. There were boxes of food supplies stacked along the walls. The kitchen had piles of jangling pots, pans, and all manner of tools—all of which had been recently salvaged from various recycling and secondhand shops.

Josef could still not be dissuaded, "Comfort be damned! As long as there is enough room to work, we will work."

Nearly destitute from its start-up, Josef and Steve had to bring in some revenue. If their restaurant failed, as had already been discussed, they would eat the massive supply of start-up food and hole up in Cigarette's until the police came to throw them out on the streets or in jail. Then, when the authorities came for them, they would poison and kill themselves on the spot. It was unlikely that they would carry through with this plan, but they hadn't considered any other options.

In a move so bold it was nearly life threatening, they decided to give every new customer their first meal for half price. The food was great, but it was Steven's powerful charm and dedicated service that made Cigarette's memorable. Their social media exploded.

5quabbler_77 wrote:

*Pretty tough to get me outta tha house these days but I'll be back soon. Super delicious and the waiter guy was great. Five Stars. *****

ThickJawGunSlinger001 wrote:

*The pierogis remind me of something from when I was a kid except were probably even better. *****

EyyyeGotThatDooope_13 wrote:

Really good for around here. I might even come back when they stop   giving out 50% off :p ****

Advanced1ntelli6ence wrote:

Wanted to hate it. Liked it. Worth it. *****

People started arriving in droves. They were packed from lunch until late dinner. There was atmosphere in Cigarette's. Josef and Steve were madly in love, although without any employees they worked so hard that they rarely found time to express it. The profound intimacy of falling asleep in the same bed together, even if only for a few hours, with the smells of all their work in the air alongside a quiet discussion of tomorrow's plans was a spiritual experience.

Economics, however, created earthly realities that set in quickly. The food at Cigarette's was stealing potential customers from other businesses whose owners were also the fighting type.

A small group of competitors paid a local health inspector and general nuisance named Norton Rogers to bust Josef, whose food was obviously outside the norm. It had been less than a year since another coordinated string of poisonings, so Josef and Steven's timing could not have been worse. Creating one's own illicit food products had recently been equated with gross negligence. The media said that misdemeanors could mean murder, and people were alarmed.

When the inspector first arrived to "sample" the food at Cigarette's, he filled a vial with the innards of the daily special. That day the dish in question had been cabbage rolls and sausage. The entire place smelled marvelous. Norton was reminded of his own mother's cooking as he was growing up; it bought back an uncomfortable nostalgia. He thought it best to not sample the dish, regardless. Perhaps this could have been seen as creating a conflict of interest, but Norton's commitments were far beyond even that rationale. He was more genuinely afraid that a few homemade cabbage rolls might actually kill him.

The test results came back the next day and confirmed the presence of several spices not present in any of the standard-issue sauces. Norton received a search warrant the same week and presented it in dramatic fashion to Josef and Steven, who were appalled and rightfully nervous. The inspection of the facility, however, revealed hardly anything. Josef was wise enough to destroy all the evidence that would have certainly doomed the restaurant's future. All that was discovered was a mixing bowl with the residue of prohibited spices underneath Josef and Steven's bed. A forgotten late-night experiment had been tasted right before sleep postponing passion. Indeed, some foods really were aphrodisiacs and the two, slightly past their prime, experimented with every flavor. Something about the spiciest and most exotic flavors made them irresistible to one another.

Norton was almost satisfied after emailing an expensive citation to the helpless couple. To cover the fine that Cigarette's received, some of the better equipment they had purchased during the eatery's upswing was sold. So were all but two of the television table mats. What was even worse for Cigarette's was that Josef's trust had been affected. After this experience, he would only serve new and unknown customers the standard food they'd come to expect from every other restaurant in the area. He would only use preapproved ingredients for fear of losing everything that he and Steven had worked so hard for. The culmination of these changes lost many current and prospective customers.

Playing it safe was the correct move, however. Norton became infuriated when, after sending in all kinds of degenerate people he paid to try the nonstandard foods he thought Josef was still selling to the regulars, they would come out empty-handed. Norton dug through their garbage periodically, even though these findings would never have been permissible in the court system, and still found very little. Norton had wasted so much time, and the other restaurants pressuring him were not satisfied with Josef and Steven's audacity to remain open.

The fine that the local health authorities handed down was exorbitant and nearly did topple their dreams. Real reports of special sauces were still circulating around the neighborhood, and the regulars were still able to enjoy them. But in general, business didn't take off like Steven and Josef wanted. After a few slow days of grinding it out and thinking about ways to stir up some action, Josef was heading outside to toss out some prescreened passable garbage when he caught Norton sifting through the dumpster in the alley behind Cigarette's late one afternoon. He opened his back door and a few feet away saw a wide ass in ill-fitting black dress pants bent over the big green bin.

"Get the hell outta here, you bloody leech!" Josef screamed loud enough that Norton, shocked, fell backward from the container and rolled to the ground.

Still on the ground, Norton blurted out, "I should tell the authorities that you attacked me, you criminal prick!" He got to his feet in a little rolling motion, getting more dirty than necessary. Josef thought Norton resembled a wad of dough collecting flour.

"You can tell them whatever you want, you whack job, but know that before I go to jail I will make such a mess of that orb you call a body that you won't be digging through a dumpster ever again." Josef's fist was balled, but he spoke clearly with limited emotions.

"You can't threaten me! I own you and your faggot waiter!" Norton said, with a vile grin. He beat at his clothes awkwardly, attempting to brush off the filth.

This was far from the first time that someone had attempted to belittle Josef for his sexuality. Josef wasn't about to let the utterance affect him since he knew that an altercation was what Norton was after; he could sell an altercation to the precinct.

"That faggot is my husband, and the law doesn't look very kindly on hate crimes, you piece of shit. So get the hell out of here before I start taking pictures of your disgusting fat ass playing detective," Josef said, hanging a very loose middle finger a few safe feet away in front of Norton's face while he stared at him with hatred in his eyes.

"You're finished. Cigarette's is finished!" Norton said, unable to reciprocate the eye contact as he walked away stiffly, uttering a few grunts like a dejected animal.

Over the course of the argument, Steven and Sheriff William had heard Norton's hollering from inside Cigarette's. By the time they made it outside the door, they had missed most of the action and instead were disappointed to find a dirty Norton waddling away with a limp.

"Are you okay?" Steven asked, confused about what had happened.

"I'm fine … Sick little pissant … If that jowly, gray-fleshed slug doesn't die of diabetes then frosting must be a health food," replied Josef, continuing to ramble in a low, toneless drawl with Steven hanging on his shoulder. "It's like … always cornering something only to have it *disappear.* Through some tiny hole. Which would mean that the corner was only temporary, I guess … Or it never existed at all, and all the time the light was the only obstacle. We need holes I guess, I…" Josef was losing his train of thought.

"Joe! What are you talking about? Don't let him get to you! We are better than this. Let's just get back to work." Josef knew that Steven was trying to take his attention away from the problem, which he appreciated. But problems seemed to be growing lately. Staying distracted by work had usually done the trick in the past. When things were too hectic, sometimes Josef began to lose his balance.

Josef watched as William looked around the scene. He had been watching the couple reel from the incident apparently trying to surmise what had transpired. Josef saw William open his mouth for a second, as if to yell at Norton on his way down the alley, but he closed it thoughtfully instead.

William directed his attention to Steven and Josef. Steven was hugging Josef, who was barely able to return the embrace due to his vibrating anger.

"Listen, you two, I will keep an eye out for Norton. I'm not positive about why he is harassing you, so I won't write this up as a report yet. But if he bothers you again, make sure I'm the first to know, okay?"

"We definitely will … Will," replied Josef.

"Unless you would like me to follow up on this?" William asked.

"Not a chance," stated Josef, regaining some of his composure somewhat suddenly. "You just take care of real problems. We've dealt with this kind of nonsense before, and I'm sure it won't be the last time. As long as you keep eating here with us, we'll be happy. I wouldn't want something minor like this to change that."

"I would like that very much too, you guys," William said, sounding a little unprofessional.

"You're right, Joe. That guy is nothing but a leech. Forget him, and let's just carry on being fantastic, okay?" He held on to Josef again and forced a big smile. Josef could tell that Steven was trying to charm him back inside so he could cool down. It worked, and he followed the hand leading him back to his station in front of the stove.

He looked over his shoulder to be sure Norton was finally gone before closing the door. Indeed, Norton had slid out of sight, and Josef latched the door after returning inside. He took a deep breath. Then another. He thought for a minute about how ridiculous it was that he had this new enemy and laughed out loud shaking his head. His thick calloused fist slammed down on one of the aluminum shelves. The cook-wear created a brief clamor.

Steven looked back at him nervously.

"We just can't catch a break, can we?" Josef said, choosing to brush off the intensity of the moment and retie his apron, showing Steven that he was over it and it was back to business as usual.

Steven said, "Give it some time my dear."

Josef threw an overdone burger patty in the trash and was working on peeling a new one out of its cellophane wrapper. "I know, Steven. I feel that way too. We can't let ourselves get affected. He's just a damn leech. He should be pulled off my ass with a little salt and then fed to the fish." Josef threw the meat wad on the grill, and it hissed a satisfying hiss.

Chapter 13, Frequency

As always, the present day made all previous time periods seem as though they were full of nothing but the most deprived of history's simpletons. It was now laughable to think, that at various points over the last hundred years, people thought televisions would become obsolete with the increasing reliance of people on their personal computers. As it was, each year the sets continued to become larger and marketably different in terms of 3-D clarity, connectivity, modern color, texture, feel, taste, sexuality … The most appreciated new standard for consumers now was that all televisions came with free installation.

Installation was completely necessary even for the more fit television aficionado, since the carpet-like television mats were inherently heavy, fragile, and awkward. Fortunately for everyone, the mats were fluidly bendable, ensuring that even the tiniest apartment up tight flights of stairs and through sandwiched doorways was still guaranteed the largest possible rolled-on, wall-covering television mat. "Simply measure, order, and wait for the delivery of a much-deserved upgrade to your lifestyle!" is what the previously fine televisions barked at the vacant, slouching, crumb-covered beings on the receiving end. Often enough that, as one slob turned to the other slob in their barren and filthy nests, they would shrug and agree that an upgrade certainly couldn't hurt.

It was impressive how so many people who could barely afford their rent and their basic sustenance each week, somehow still managed to obtain one of these flashing behemoths. Lifetimes of stimulated consumption tended to produce these types of unglamorous miracles. Other more meaningful change was much harder to achieve and was therefore a less engaging prospect to those looking for quick fixes and cheap comforts. Of course, there were energetic visionaries whose strangeness often made them targets but also afforded them pleasures that would be unimaginable to those trapped in their cyclic safety nets. The general situation, however, reeked of the leftovers from forgotten and unfulfilled youths.

The world's most brilliant and dominant minds continuously worked on technological and informative ways to enrich the lives of all free citizens. They insisted that society was progressing, always moving toward social development. There was a way to reanimate any extinct animal. There was the technology to sweep the oceans clean. There was clean energy available for all, at a fraction of the cost that the current corporations charged. But politics blocked the way like a frozen glass door. It also slowly picked off the bright minds and lured the frustrated into increasingly consumer-driven pursuits. You couldn't say that the system was archaic, since even in early America there was unbridled progress. More correctly, the system was broken, manipulated past the point of return like a cracked and overstretched elastic band.

The average person was powerless beneath laws created to secure the wealthy. Most simply tried to survive under the radar and hoped that there were enough like-minded people to ensure their basic well-being. Fairness hadn't existed since the dawn of humanity, and some became infuriated with seeing generation after generation willing to accept powerlessness with smiling faces, when no one seemed to believe any of the reasons for the stalemate. It was as if the untouchably avaricious were able to enjoy themselves more by pretending that the proletariat were content barely hanging on each day and praying for something better. For the most part, they were correct. People thrived on hope. Despair was not as profitable.

***

Recycling everything possible and refining the scrap had become major business. Not solely because the world had run low on resources and the remaining areas rich in metals, fuels, and minerals were more remote and more inaccessible than ever, but the real problem was the refining and transporting of new ore and raw materials of every kind. The cost of labor to finish the goods was, in the end, passed on to the consumers, who were not willing to pay for a level of quality they no longer valued.

Again, much of this problem was attributed to fuel and transportation costs. It was more economical to pay people to rip through acres of waste and melt their findings down to be reused. It also made people feel as though they were saving the planet, which had grown so paranoid lately that disaster capitalism had become a household word. Workers were not actually saving the planet but salvaging, recycling, and refining was huge business, and those with jobs sorting through trash were happy to be getting paid. Salvage was all based on material type and weight. This made for a big difference between good weeks and bad weeks for those hand-sorting scrap, since sometimes they found copper wire, while other times it was days and days of rotten food and plastics. Those working the conveyor belts sorting predetermined electronic waste were paid hourly. Their days dragged on in impoverished tedium.

Planning the obsolescence of new goods kept the cycle of waste fresh. Manufacturing in the US was booming from the reuse of a few centuries of importing. Now cheap, unnecessary goods were exchanged with other countries worldwide or traded with desperate nations for more valuable resources. Super centers were located literally right next to the manufacturing plants. This blew away even the most conservative ideals of inbound logistics from the past. These manufacturing plants were logically located as close as possible to the refuse stations, and most people simply didn't care as long as they got theirs at the end of the line.

The most recent estimates were alarming: the United States' landfills were accepting nearly half a billion tonnes of solid waste per year. The Environmental Protection Agency (EPA), once an organization fought for by passionate environmental activists, was now only a thin gelatinous shell around massive privately owned waste-management companies. It was hard for anyone to stage successful protests against these organizations now, because not only did they employ so many people, but if they were to stop their current pace, the pollution, accumulation of hazardous materials, and backlog of solid waste would make entire cities unlivable. For some areas of the country it could literally become lethal if the thousands of refuse workers were to suddenly stop.

***

Kalvin had worked in the local recycling plant since he was seventeen. He had gotten a few promotions and lived comfortably, but he loathed what he did. Jesse worked on the complete other end of the spectrum selling insurance. They both wanted desperately to escape the paths they had chosen, but meeting up to get drunk together was as close to an effort as they intended to get.

Kalvin sat on one of the plastic chairs outside Cigarette's and glanced at the beautiful diamond-shaped patch of sky poking through the clouds. The rich blue emptiness contrasted by wispy cloudy streaks didn't give him the feeling of doomsday. If anything it was boring stillness. Perhaps it was even pleasant.

"So I think I'll quit the line," Kalvin stated blankly, referring to his job at the recycling plant. Really he wasn't on "the line" anymore and actually sorted the more hazardous materials while clad in a highly efficient safety suit. This was a far cry from the years he had spent beside a conveyor belt sorting rubbish. He still referred to his job as "the line" to conjure sympathy. He stared off into the distance waiting for the pills he had just tossed down his throat to take effect.

Jesse wasted no time vocalizing his disapproval.

"You make me sad," he said. "People feeling sorry for you must give you some kind of superpower, because you just take whatever's the worst decision you can make at the time and go with it."

Kalvin wasn't offended but still cared to talk out the decision he had been mulling over as if it had already been made. As if the drugs hadn't just made him melancholic enough to blame his employment for his current feelings. As if it wasn't just talk.

"I can't be a fucking 'nosey' my whole life, man! There is no way I can handle one more day in that fucking suit, Jesse!" He raised his voice, finally, temporarily charged with a lifetime of minor frustrations and substantial failures. He was alarmed by how loud he had been, wondering if he was too high and was getting out of bounds. Then he wondered if he was too high and was imagining that he was out of bounds. Finally he just felt pleasantly strange and numb and didn't care much either way.

A "nosey" was common slang for the recycling workers' hazardous materials suits. Every employee in the recycling pits wore these eerie insect-like helmets for the entire day except for when they broke for lunch. The dark UV-protective eyeholes flashed a chrome sheen if you caught them at the perfect angle, ensuring that you never saw any of your fellow employee's expressions. The front of the mask had a bulge where the airtight filtration mask was placed over the mouth and nose with a small amplifier built inside for communication. On the sides, two small fans gently circulated and cooled the air contained within. The helmets made the wearer look like a lifeless and morose alien.

The mask's functionality was very good for the dangerous work it was designed for. It kept the employees safe from the sun, toxic gases, and hazardous particles, while also serving as a deflection shield. Straps were tightened around the top of the head and from the chin to the back of the head. Then the mask's front was swung down, replacing the user's face with a horrifying mouthless orb. Two more straps were tightened to secure the oxygen and air filtration mask, and the remaining length of these were secured to Velcro at the shoulders. A light Kevlar jacket was zipped up over all of the straps and kept any participant safe for as long as they were encapsulated.

Kalvin had worked behind his own mask for eight years. The job had seemed like a fantastic and legitimate opportunity when he'd begun. There was even a tube in the mask that popped in your mouth when you leaned your head back allowing you to suck some water out of it if you were thirsty while you worked. It could be a comfortable and healthy job. At the time, it had seemed like the best thing since opposable thumbs, but the job was a trap and the safety of the mask was one of many contrived angles to retain employees.

Maintaining the mask was an employee's responsibility, and with all of the tiny moving parts and the often-rough nature of the job, it broke down constantly. The replacement parts themselves were not overly expensive, but the time and expertise it took to repair them, for those without serious spare time and ingenuity, were quite costly. You had to work with a "nosey" on even while your mask was being repaired; in the meantime you had to rent a company mask. Due to company safety protocol and the problems caused by people trying to cut corners by fixing the masks themselves, each mask that had been marked as broken needed to be inspected before it was allowed back in the workplace. There was a fee for this service too, and each transition was monitored closely.

Eight years had passed, and Kalvin had nothing to show for them except his clean-shaven face required by the safety officers to ensure an airtight fit for his mask. He was able to afford his own lonely apartment and his own food and drinks. In Kalvin's case, only the most basic food was essential, while a good quantity of drugs and drink used up the rest of his allowance.

"There is nothing I have done in my entire life that makes me as depressed as the eight hours a day I spend in that suit," Kalvin stated, lighting another smoke. Once a month or so he would get like this, and by the next morning the concoction of amnesia-inducing substances he had ingested made the depression disappear and replaced it with a kind of empty confusion.

"If you are really as unhappy as you want me to believe, then you should have been looking for another job while you still have the security of this one. If you quit now, there is no way they will take you back when your job search dies. And it will—there's nothing out there."

"I don't care, my man," Kalvin said, finishing off a can of ginseng energy malt. "I will never go back to sorting. I genuinely don't care what happens, as long as I never go back to that next Monday. I would rather do anything. I mean, I hope to find something interesting to do and make some money so I can be comfortable. Yeah? Just like you. But if I strike out and have to start stealing shit or selling drugs I'd even be happier doing that than working in the pits."

"I'd give you a week at either of those occupations," Jesse replied, referring to the highly competitive and deadly thieving and dealing trades.

The reality of this statement was too much to overcome. Instead, Kalvin decided to rant a bit, hoping to find his point along the journey.

"Do you think I ever owned anything, my brother? No. Nothing. I have shared an apartment with a mixture of at times two, sometimes three other transient losers for more than eight years. They eat my food, use my toilet paper, and for my generosity I have been robbed and abandoned three times. The last time, some useless goofball asshole even stole my socks. I had just done laundry, came here for a lunch on my day off, and I guess the warm little sock-pile was simply too tempting. That place where you live the, whatever, 17th Street Projects, or whatever? They are owned—and I'm not kidding—by a subsidiary of US Waste. It's ironic that I don't live there too. And my parents didn't own shit either! They leased their car and rented their apartment. I sold my mom's jewelry to buy an urn for her funeral. Fuck. *Fuck!* Whatever. We are chickens, we are hyenas, we are cannibalizing our dead. I might as well accept my reality and whatever fate brings my way."

"Well, that fate will be death. In three weeks. Don't quit your job, Kalvin," Jesse replied. "I know life is frustrating. I feel the same way a lot, but I have also heard most of these details before. Pretty much every month. The rerun gets predictable after a while."

Kalvin's mind was wandering now and was getting a tingly vibe of druggy pleasure. He was more than happy to ignore Jesse's pleas.

"I just thank God that I haven't screwed up enough to enjoy the gooey miracle of having children yet. I think I would end up feeling suicidally guilty for dooming some poor innocent life by causing it to be born here. I've yet to have anyone suggest, to my satisfaction, a respectable way to escape this place."

"You're killing me." Jesse moved around uncomfortably in his chair. "I just want to relax and plan something fun to do this weekend. Maybe get out of the city for a bit, like we always talk about."

"Realistically it's more likely we will end up nursing hangovers again. But I agree, let's catch a movie or something," Kalvin concluded.

They both paused for a second. Kalvin glanced at Cerberus chewing on a bone. The dog was busying himself just out of his reach. It made him happy that Cerberus looked so content.

"I'm hungry," Kalvin said, dashing his cigarette butt out in the jar of rocks. "Let's get something to eat."

"Sounds good." Said Jesse, getting up from the table.

Kalvin got up slowly too, content that he'd changed Jesse's emotional direction. He really wanted Jesse to be happy; he had so much potential. If only the world could have been ready for someone smart and caring who could make good decisions for its betterment.

Kalvin thought about some of the books written by men of the past who thought they'd known what the future would hold. Where was the calamity every visionary predicted? Where are we right now, Nostradamus? Why is this so easy, Orwell? Instead of anything exciting and wild and cataclysmic happening, society's progress seemed to Kalvin to be more like aging. It was all such a slow process of loss.

Kalvin walked over to unclip Cerberus from his run and put him back on the post near his bed. Once he had the dog off his leash, he reached down near his left ankle and pulled a light pink pill out of his sock. He knocked it back, swallowing it with whatever gluey saliva he had left in his mouth. Jesse had apparently been watching Kalvin as he began massaging his throat and composing himself.

"You're a self-fulfilling prophecy, dude. How long have you been waiting around to die? Because I haven't hit that lineup yet."

Kalvin was the one to get irritated this time.

"You know what?" Kalvin said. "My reality suits me just fine."

He reached down to pet Cerberus as he passed him. Cerberus tensed his neck muscles to elevate his head higher, participating happily in the exchange and oblivious to the pointless rationalization of the two grumpy, aging drunks. They were so wrapped up in themselves that they failed to notice the pup follow them inside and settle down into his closet before the door slowly closed behind them.

"Nosey"

Chapter 14, the Gates

William and Kalvin had met prior to Cigarette's bringing their lives together for a second time. A cold November night with a freezing layer of fog on the ground had created the first opportunity. William had been the first officer on the scene of the car accident during his night shift. It was four in the morning and accidents around this time were generally of the worst nature. When Will approached the outdated automobile, which was now a shredded pile of twisted metal and sharp, scattered fragments of plastic, he was skeptical of the occupants' survival. The vehicle had careened off the entrance of one overpass before spinning around backward and crashing into a median on a second overpass below. If the car hadn't been hung up on the railing it would have added another thirty-foot plummet and certain death to the total of the scene in the grisly-gray river below.

William reached the second overpass quickly, after calling for an ambulance, and to his surprise Kalvin was still conscious. Kalvin's mouth opened as William approached him, but only a low moan came out. His arm was pinned messily outside the car window between two pieces of the door that had enclosed on it like a pair of thick, dull scissors. The car was situated so that it forced Kalvin's eyes, although barely open, to stay trained on William as he ran toward him.

Unforgettably for Captain William, there was a white cigarette butt still burning a few feet away from the blood pool below Kalvin's suspended and nearly severed arm. William stomped it out immediately. *He can't have been pinned for very long*, was William's rapid conclusion as he arrived at the side of the car. Even if this deduction was correct, the amount of blood loss was alarming, as it often was in scenes like this. William needed to focus, though: shock was clearly setting in quickly for the victim.

"An ambulance is on the way, son. We are going to get you out of here, and you are going to be fine. Now, just try to hang on for me, okay?"

"Get … get me out. Just … get me out … Please." Kalvin begged repeatedly, and in varying tones and arrangements.

"When you remember this moment, you are going to want to remember yourself being strong, okay? What is your name?"

"Kalvin."

"Okay, Kalvin, this is it. I'm going to get you out of here, and our friends at the hospital are going to have you in good shape in no time. Just stay with me."

Kalvin breathed in deeply and nodded in understanding. His free arm had been making a small gyrating motion, and it came to rest on the wet asphalt. William opened the accident kit he had lugged down the hill with him from his black ghost-car.

"Here we go, Kalvin."

William stationed two small automated jacks, one between the car door and the frame and one between the frame and the asphalt. He quickly made a tourniquet for Kalvin's arm while the little jacks went to work. The door handle popped open first, and then the door was lifted off Kalvin's arm. Kalvin screamed and began to pull his arm back toward his body like a dead snake. William gently but firmly seized the blood-soaked hand.

"Try to stay still, Kalvin," William said as he began forcefully wrapping the tourniquet. He used his gloves and the sleeve of his jacket to brush the majority of the broken glass out of the way. Time was more important than perfection, and after a few quick swipes he focused back on Kalvin.

"Now try to relax. I'm going to pull you out slowly. I can hear the ambulance; it's your lucky day, alright? Here we go."

He rolled Kalvin on his back with both arms in front of him like a mummy. William then grabbed Kalvin's shoulders and pulled him out of the wreckage and Kalvin winced out a fairly loud and unintelligible sound. William kept pulling and soon had him free of the car.

"We made it, Kalvin. You're going to be alright," William reassured him. When the ambulance arrived, he was already pulling bits of glass out of Kalvin's face as he drifted dangerously close to unconsciousness.

William watched for a moment as the EMTs arrived. Kalvin's spine checked out, and it appeared that most of the damage he had sustained was to his arm and shoulder. He'd probably had his arm outside the window when the car had rolled. Kalvin wasn't paying attention to the questions the nurses were asking him but managed to look at William and say, "Thank you," in not much more than a whisper.

The EMTs lifted the stretcher up and began rolling it away.

"You're welcome, Kalvin; take care of yourself now," William said and walked back to inspect the vehicle.

Even though he was never breathalyzed, Kalvin's intoxication was more than obvious—with the various bottles of pills in the backseat of the wreck, and with the overwhelming smell of liquor coming from him as he had screamed in pain. Sheriff

William followed through with pressing charges. Kalvin never served any time in jail, but he lost his license and suffered some serious financial consequences.

In the years since, William had been silently watching as Kalvin rode his bike to Cigarette's and mixed alcohol, pills, and a little food "safely." William assumed that Kalvin was high every time he saw him drinking in a booth or smoking on the patio behind Cigarette's. If Kalvin was inside, he would often leave shortly after he sat down. If William passed Kalvin when approaching the bar to pay, or to use the bathroom, he would always smile and say, "Hi, Kalvin."

Kalvin was usually wearing massive dark glasses or would look up through squinting dark eyes and smile at him. The "Hello, Captain" and the salute were always genuine, but it was easy for William to tell that the happiness was not. William had yet to see Kalvin drink and drive after his accident, which had been nearly four years earlier. He also knew that Kalvin had gotten his license back recently and that the likelihood of Kalvin making smart and safe decisions decreased with each hazy day he continued to live.

***

Kalvin and Jesse had both finished eating a thick turkey vegetable stew complete with rich sour cream and cheese biscuits in one of Cigarette's booths. They were full and had been drinking, beer for beer, for the better part of two hours on the pleasant, warm Friday afternoon. Captain William and Cynthia had just entered and walked by the table where they were sitting.

Kalvin nodded to them pleasantly. "Good evening, guys. The stew tonight was off the charts; I suggest one of you give it a try."

William replied, "Well, it smells fantastic in here, so I might have to take you up on that."

"Good evening," Jesse said to Cynthia with a smile.

"Good evening, boys," Cynthia returned the courtesy pleasantly.

The couple passed the two men and settled in a few booths away.

Kalvin still had his jacket around his shoulders, hiding his scarred arm, pretending that he wasn't uncomfortably warm. He and Jesse had sunk into their booth seats. Jesse was noticeably more intoxicated than Kalvin, which was due purely to tolerance. Not only had Kalvin downed the same amount of watery, cold, corn-syrup-base golden draft, but he was also riding the tingly buzz of his romantically assembled pill concoction.

They were having a good time, laughing about mutual friends with their own various pitfalls and idiosyncrasies. They felt young. They felt like they looked cool. They felt present, and it felt good.

Kalvin decided to attempt a joke. "So there's this old fella that can't get it up, and it's his and his wife's fiftieth anniversary or whatever." He jumped right into the joke, and Jesse listened attentively. "For the last ten or so years they have still been on and off each other every month or so, but every time the mood strikes them the good old guy rubs on some cream to help him get it up. All is well."

"All is indeed well," interjected Jesse, with a big closed-mouth smirk.

"Right, right," Kalvin said. His face looked bright, sharp, and angular. "Everything's peachy in retirement-sex paradise."

Jesse loved this, and laughed a little too loudly.

Kalvin continued.

"So they're at home, and they've wrapped up dinner. His wife is getting ready in the bedroom, and he's in the bathroom going to rub on his woody-wax, but he can't find the little jar." He broke for a second for effect. "So he starts freaking out, and eventually his wife comes in smiling ear to ear. She asks him what is taking so long, and he tells her the problem. But she just looks at him with a huge obnoxious smile. 'Why the hell are you so happy?' he asks. 'Without my cream, there's no way we are doing any celebrating tonight!' 'I'm not happy, Ted. In fact, I'm pissed,' she says, with this huge ridiculous grin. 'And if you leave that stuff beside my face moisturizer again, I'm gonna snap that damn thing right off your body.'"

Jesse snickered. "Haw, haw. Not bad, I guess, Kal. Pretty PG, and your delivery could use some work."

He judged the joke more critically than Kalvin thought he would.

"What?" Kalvin said, still playing along. "That's comic gold. They're both old, forgetful buggers … Come on board, buddy. That's good stuff."

"You just like it because you have such a close relationship with Viagra," Jesse said, a little loose-lipped because of his inebriation.

"Come on now, mate, let's leave my unit out of this," Kalvin said, not appreciating that the joke might be heading his way.

"You know you wouldn't even need that stuff if you would drop all that other unnecessary … medicine," Jesse said.

This conversation came up nearly every time they met lately. They had arrived at some kind of basic truce where Jesse could say whatever he wanted about it, because he loved Kalvin and he refused to hide his concern. In return for the concern, Kalvin went ahead and did whatever he felt like regardless.

"Hey, even if I get the dink droops—which doesn't happen that often, by the way—popping something to fix that and to have twenty-five minutes of sex is just as alright with me as popping something else to fix my mood. Almost interchangeable, really. I know I need to work on it, Jess … and wean off a bit more but, like I've said, I'm just a recreational user, buddy."

Jesse sat up straighter in his seat.

"See, even the fact that you said twenty-five minutes of sex makes the whole thing seem so methodical and cold. There is no way you can enjoy all of life's experiences to the depth that someone not doped up can, if your self-medication keeps you vibrating on only one frequency like that. Even if you're changing meds or going on or off them, you're always so aware of this, that frequency or whatever. You have chosen this as your spice, and controlling that is a lot of work, dude. You should allow things to just happen sometimes. See what life is like when given to chance."

Kalvin leaned in close to Jesse and controlled the tone of his voice as if they were still maintaining a fun conversation.

"How can you talk to me about perseverance? Honestly, Jesse, you have been at the exact same job for ten years of your used-to-be-fortunate life, and you hate it. There isn't much available for someone without the education you couldn't afford, is there? With the skills I have handling hazmats, I could quit tomorrow, go completely sideways on drugs for three days, and get hired after a piss test a week later. Perhaps I wouldn't make as much as I do now, but if I needed the change, people are *waiting* for me."

He leaned back and reached in his jacket pocket and held up a small rectangular translucent-green plastic prism with a cotton swab stuffed in the top, presumably so it wouldn't rattle when he walked. He continued as Jesse averted his eyes to look at his beer.

"I hate my job, but it is more legitimate than yours have been, and I know that's unfair. You tell me to keep my job and maybe you're right. But then these little beauties"—he shook the box, which made a few muffled clicks—"these help me tolerate the grind. If some other 'frequency' helps me think up a better plan next week, then I'm all for it." He placed the little box back in his pocket without thinking about exactly how close a known police officer was. "And believe me, sometimes you have to ride out an unwanted wave during some shitty e-conference, and whether you're sober or not, it's going to suck the same amount but for different reasons. When it comes to that, I've been able to stay sober for my entire career. So don't tell me about perseverance, dude."

Jesse looked like a scolded dog. "I get that," he said to Kalvin, in a tone of surrender. "And it's surprising to me that you stay looking so healthy and in shape. You must be doing something right."

"I'm sure my liver and kidneys would disagree," Kalvin said plainly.

Jesse laughed. "That's true, but I'm starting to get fatter all the time, and I'm sure my insides don't look great from all the garbage I'm ingesting either."

Kalvin perked up a bit again. "The craziest thing is that the average person's daily intake of black market pharmaceuticals is less expensive than buying high-end healthy groceries. I was watching this show saying that this may be why so many people are choosing instead to eat garbage and feel good from self-medicating."

"I know," replied Jesse. "I've even considered asking you what I should be taking to help me slim down a bit."

They both looked out into the adjacent yard full of broken plastic remains from some traffic control equipment that had been left there by road workers the previous night. Now the orange and yellow beacons, pylons, and dividers, every last one of them, had been smashed to bits so small that particles would likely remain on the sandy surface for years. The drunks and mischievous children always did an adequate job of destroying everything man-made and abandoned when it drew their attention. Kalvin liked seeing the destruction. He thought Mother Nature must smile around her vandals as they helped expedite the reclamation of what will always be hers.

"Well, as long … I mean, as *enlightened* as this conversation has been, I'm feeling better than I did when I got here," Kalvin said.

"Me too, dude," Jesse replied, taking another deep gulp of his beer. "Thanks for meeting up."

Chapter 15, Nothing But Time

Jesse had been a good student when he was in his teens. He had graduated with honors from high school and was presented with a small gold-colored "honors" medal made out of some kind of cheap metal on a shiny but roughly cut ribbon. He still had a picture of himself in the blue graduation gown with his arms around his mother and father. The picture had stayed in his living room because the three of them looked so happy that it brightened his spirits. It had also been rescued from the garbage a few times. On dark and tired mornings, he sometimes looked at that picture as he woke and imagined his medal as a noose.

Sometimes he thought that marijuana might have had an effect on his aspirations. As an adult he forgot to attempt any kind of experiment that may have proved this theory wrong or right. Since the summer after graduation, his occasional pot smoking had turned into a daily ritual. He couldn't imagine living without it.

The parties he had attended back then made it seem as though nothing but the greatest of opportunities awaited him. Morning hangovers were easy to deal with then. A little food, an energy drink, a couple of tokes ... no problem. What was everyone whining about? Doing what he wanted to do all the time seemed to be the best way to suck the greatest rewards out of the one life that he had been given.

He believed so strongly in his potential when he was younger. Self-confidence had opened a lot of doors for him. After his first summer of being barely employed and enjoying this type of wild freedom, Jesse was already bored. He was happy that he'd been previously accepted into college so he had something to do. Throughout the summer he considered not going back to school because he was having so much fun, but in the fall it was a relieving option. He rode off to college and experienced much of what he had imagined. This included many more parties, unremarkable passing grades, and some time spent at the gym. The time he put into getting in shape was about a quarter of the

228

time he spent trolling for girls. He considered that there were prerequisites to success, but still he didn't change his approach and the results didn't bring much luck.

Jesse received his Bachelors of Administration degree four years later and was a little surprised that he had made it. The entire summer after his last semester was spent applying for jobs and attending interviews, but for some reason opportunities weren't jumping up to greet the shiny new graduate. Actually, the jobs that were "waiting" for him post-grad had lineups of people applying for them. None of the companies he really wanted to work for seemed to have any openings. Inexperience was a difficult thing to shed, and his motivation for the most desirable positions waned when he found out the starting wages were so low.

Some jobs were available that paid well, but they required extremely heavy time commitments. These jobs also required almost no real decision-making or creative skills. The pressure finally mounted, and as his financial situation became crucial he decided to sign a contract across the table from a glum-looking man in a poorly fitting suit. He was given his duties at the small corporate insurance company that was now his home, and he consistently carried them out adequately. He would usually complete his duties early and then work on ideas that might bring the company more revenue or save them time. Jesse's ambition was not well received, however, and he was reprimanded for going beyond his general duties.

Money began to roll in and out of Jesse's life in a somewhat satisfying fashion. He had, for a short time, stopped partying when he was "interview fresh," but it didn't take him long to settle back into a heavy daily ritual. It had become his favorite part of each weekday, and he was insanely irritable without it. He was so bored without it. He got sore without it. He was constantly trying to find the perfect pivot point between alcohol, caffeine, and THC. Some days he found it for an hour or two, and that achievement had become good enough to get by. This type of limbo had become so ingrained in him that the years had somehow turned into a decade.

Jesse had met a girl who shared his interest in escapism, right after he landed the reasonable job with the little company near the bottom floor of the big office tower. There seemed to be room for advancement even if his duties weren't overly satisfying, and his radiant optimism must have been magnetic. Life felt very good for a short while. The only problem he really had was leaving his bed for the desk every morning, after he'd done his best to enjoy each night. Eventually Jesse began to feel excessively tired all the time. In the mornings he begrudgingly chugged coffee and then hopped on the train to arrive at the same place that now infected his dreams. Once inside, he saw the same people, and they grew indifferent to each other's presence quickly. He stared at a screen for eight hours, and each hour was subdivided into impossibly long sections.

Bleak thoughts bounced around, trapped in his mind, when he arrived home each day. On the weekends he made some emotional progress. He would take his girlfriend out so they could enjoy themselves in the city. They would eat at some nearby reasonably priced restaurants and were usually disappointed with the food. Then they would watch a movie, but their tastes in film were so incredibly different that one of them always ended up dissatisfied. They would then get quite drunk and stoned. The prospect of Monday still haunted all these experiences, except when he was at the furthest end of his avoidance.

This cycle seemed tolerable enough until the couple's needs grew. Their tiny apartment began to feel like a cell, and they couldn't afford to do anything new. Near the end of their relationship, even the basic foods that they made themselves and had previously enjoyed brought no pleasure. They expected the maturing of their relationship to make everything better. They expected rich complexity, potency, and sweetness, but somewhere along the way the cork had slipped and spoiled it. Perhaps the ingredients were never very good to begin with. All they were left with had no use or value, and moreover was a burden to even throw away.

When his girlfriend left him, it was at the height of his pre-breakup depression. Finally his loneliness helped bring all his feelings to the surface, and he was able to accept them. Not much else had changed. He was still in the same small apartment and at the same job, but he realized how much pain he was in. He chose to replace his ex's absence with some new electronics and a copious amount of liquor and marijuana, knowing that it wouldn't solve his problems but also realizing that he didn't care. He no longer felt the need to suppress anything he felt for someone else's sake, and so he let go of his controls.

Jesse had been left with one thing that hadn't already been inherently his after the breakup: a piece of advice that hurt him deeply and seemed to circle his thoughts every time he felt exhausted and angry with the world. His former girlfriend had said, "It isn't strange to me that you are mad at the world, Jesse, but nothing is fair. Nothing. Fairness is a weak fabrication. But with all your blessings you don't have the right to be angry. That bitterness will poison your potential, and it will be too late for you to change. You could have done better for us."

Then she left. At the time he had neither the heart nor the wit to respond. He just went to the couch, smoked a big bowl of dope, and cried. After that night he started to crumble. He only thought about the past. Times, years ago, when he remembered being happy. It was awfully difficult to accept the loss of that feeling of invincibility that he'd had when he was young. He still couldn't decipher if his decreasing testosterone was to blame for the way he had been feeling. The e-subscription he had to his favorite men's magazine had been telling him this for a while. Or perhaps it was just the inadequacy issues left behind from his recent breakup, and he'd actually felt better before? Maybe it was just the overwhelming sense of dread he got when he considered a future of any kind. He had come to the conclusion that it was indeed a trifecta of these facts: a perfect, inescapable blend of hopelessness.

The thing that made his present situation unbearable was the bitter layer of guilt he tasted when he considered how much worse off the majority of the world was compared to him. Whenever he reached this dark corner of his thoughts, he would become paralyzed, unable to do anything with any more intention than just going through the motions of his life already set in place. Go to work. Feel lost. Eat. Lie motionless. Drink some booze. Struggle to sleep. Smoke some weed. What does it matter? Get groceries. Attempt to clean up the house. Cry a bit on the floor watching the glow of the television shine on the dirty linoleum. Whatever.

The growing stagnancy of his life after the breakup was another manageable low, but things really began to sour after the company Jesse worked for went through its second management change. It had merged with another larger company, and now Jesse didn't know anyone higher up the ladder. He was approached with cold, distant suspicion by his new boss. The interest on his student loan rose because he hadn't finished paying it off in the allotted time. His bills just kept growing, and even his appliances began to break down. All these occurrences seemed to him to be more than coincidental. Life was out to get him. Nowhere else that was hiring offered any potential to bring in more cash than he was already making, so he stayed put. He was stuck.

It blew Jesse's mind that his life consisted of such a seemingly hopeless conundrum. When he was enjoying himself, at the bar with Kalvin or when he was with his friends during weekend adventures into the nearby hills, doing a bit of hiking and doing a bit of substance abuse, he felt great. It was there that he remembered his exhilarating ambition. He always felt that he could see three steps ahead into his own marvelous opportunities and knew, right then, all the things he wanted to accomplish in order to mine a hole into his future.

But then he would inevitably return to work each Monday, return to his apartment and to the general boring, dusty desks of his life. Soon the motivation disappeared and was replaced with fatigue. He began to feel too tired to venture out of his home even on the weekends and started visiting only a handful of familiar stores within close proximity. To battle the fatigue, he suddenly had this new desire for every type of instant gratification he could justify. He had become a dud of all the potential energy that was never released and expired. He was growing desperate.

Above all things, even above Jesse's self-pity, guilt was triumphing and directing his life. When Jesse walked home from the bus and saw the homeless people and vagrants, it felt like he needed to thank whatever abusive hand was still feeding him his scraps. He felt like this hand was the culmination of some untouchable corporate government, limiting everyone's opportunities yet sparing him from absolute impoverishment. His lack of motivation certainly didn't help, but neither did staying constantly familiar with the horrors of the world that had been given to him. He saw every realistic and graphic detail on his immense television, and this type of sadness was also hiding in every book and article he spent his time perusing. Staring at a screen and trying to unlock some secret to bettering the whole world took away from any personal ambition that might have actually culminated into something tangible. He didn't deserve anything more than he already had. He was that lucky.

Chapter 16, Blood Sucker

As Norton approached the side door of Cigarette's, he noticed a rusty tomato sauce can that had been cut in half and filled with stones. It was meant for cigarette butts, and it was doing its job. The can was nearly full of butts, along with a few pieces of gum, bits of paper, and other consumable discards. He wondered if there was any health code that this was in breach of. Most places purchased closed receptacles for their entryway disposals, and Norton felt that this old can was just another example of Josef and Steve's corner-cutting. What if a child from the street smoked a leftover cigarette butt? What if the gum or half-eaten mints attracted vermin? Surely a closed receptacle was the only healthy option. He would have to bring this up at his next meeting.

Norton passed by Cerberus, who stared up at him content-looking and panting lightly. He considered the dog disgusting and had suggested this as a health concern before, but dogs were allowed in most restaurants and there was little he could do to change this. Norton scuffed some gravel in Cerberus's direction, making the dog whine and pull back. The threat was not enough to make Cerberus try to get up, though, and none of the rocks ended up hitting him.

"Filthy piece of trash," Norton said to the dog.

As Norton entered Cigarette's, he saw Aadir and Anna turn their heads. Their strange type was easy for him to recognize, and he certainly didn't like them. The feeling was likely mutual, and they returned to their conversation more or less disregarding his presence. He approached the bar and leaned on it immediately. The walk from his car had been an uncomfortable undertaking this time.

Fucking humidity, he thought, and he wiped his brow with the back of his hand.

Norton could see Steven's reflection in the mirror that had been hung in such a way that those in the kitchen could keep an eye on the cash register area. Norton banged the service bell a couple times and could see Steven looking irritated as he saw Norton's reflection in the mirror. He stood there impatiently picking food out of his teeth with his tongue and leaning on the bar. He could see Steven setting up a teapot and some cups on a platter. Norton continued sucking on his teeth with the odd smack and slurp trying to get whatever leftover processed, salty, and sweet morsels were still floating about in his maw. He found it interesting that the gelatinous and buttery things he would eat needed so much work to dig out. It was like a race against time trying to get it all down before the inevitable sickening feeling came as his body struggled to reduce the food into fat and plaque.

Steven finally came around the corner.

"Hello, Norton, what can I do for y—" was all he managed to get out before Norton cut him off without even looking at his face.

"I need to talk to Josef," Norton said, as he readjusted himself with a grunt of displeasure. Norton wasn't sure if Josef had noticed his entrance, but he didn't want to talk to Steven because he always made him feel uncomfortable. Thankfully, Josef came then, wiping his hands with a ragged white cloth.

"What do you want?" Josef asked Norton in an exhausted monotone.

"Hello, Josef. I see that you're still cooking with illegal ingredients."

Instead of looking at Norton, Josef turned to Steven and smiled. "I couldn't do that, you know? You would never allow it."

Norton was impervious to this type of sarcasm. "I have come to watch all the meals you serve tonight and take samples of every one."

"What!" yelled Josef, throwing his rag on the ground. "You can't interfere with my business, and you sure as hell can't bother my customers. If you didn't notice already, Sheriff William is here, and he enforces the *actual* law, not your made-up bullshit."

Norton had not noticed William and Cynthia sitting in the corner booth. He generally tried to avoid eye contact with everyone in the restaurants he monitored, and this time it seemed to have been a mistake. He turned to confirm that indeed the sheriff was sitting there.

"Fine, I guess I will just do a random sample of some of your sauces then, if you don't mind."

"Of course I mind!" shouted Josef. "You have been in here twice this week, doing the same thing! This is harassment!"

Everyone could hear this outburst, and Norton liked that he was getting a reaction out of Josef.

Steven grabbed the back of Josef's shoulders in an attempt to calm him down.

Kalvin, who was sitting in the nearest booth, piped up. "You want me to toss this clown out, Josef?"

Josef bent down to pick up the rag he had previously tossed, "Hey, hey, hey ... Don't sweat it," he said, with a gesture of relaxation and open arms. "All you need to worry about is paying for dinner! That's all you need to do for me today. Just enjoy your food and relax. There is no problem here."

"There is always a problem here," Norton said.

Josef turned his back to Norton, scowling deeply. "I'm working. If you want something, don't talk to me in front of my customers. Come to the back, and tell me what it is."

Norton didn't budge. "I want to test your food," he replied. "Perhaps I wouldn't need to bother your customers if you were abiding by the regulations and not always sneaking around. I can smell the difference; whatever you are working on in the back could not possibly be any of your options." Norton asserted himself in a voice just loud enough that everyone could hear. His words were very intentional, as if he was watching himself on camera.

"I don't know what the hell you are talking about, and I don't care," Josef muttered, as he walked briskly back toward the kitchen.

Norton didn't like this and wished to recapture Josef's attention.

"I am a professional!" Norton nearly yelled. "I just need to take one *look* at whatever you're cooking back there and I could tell *instantly* if it was adulterated. Every damn thing I smell in here is illegal. You are just sneaking it past me! I don't know what the hell you're putting in your food this time, but you are endangering all these people and I am going to close you down."

Norton was standing on his own now, no longer leaning on the bar, and he was pointing and waving his arms around while bent at the waist awkwardly.

"I have told you enough times that you cannot make ingredients, of any kind, in a public restaurant. All ingredients must be purchased from an FDA-approved company."

Norton felt he had momentum now and that perhaps someone was listening to him so he continued grandstanding.

"You may also choose to have your own proprietary ingredients and sauces tested and approved in bulk then packaged appropriately and used immediately after opening."

He quickly glanced over his shoulder and no one seemed to be acknowledging Norton's speech which made him even angrier. He felt like a ghost.

Steven passed by with a little tea set, which he set down in front of William. The tea and coffee cups that Cigarette's used were a variety of different patterns, shapes, and sizes. They had all been picked up at garage sales, yard sales, and thrift shops. William thanked him when the tray was set down, but his eyes were trained on Norton.

Norton observed the mismatched tea set, and this inconsistency infuriated him; one of the cups even had a small chip on the side. He knew, however, that there was really nothing he could do about this and that Cigarette's, in fact, was just one of many small restaurants that had chosen to take this frugal approach to their dishware in order to stay afloat.

Josef then returned from the kitchen and had seemingly composed himself.

"I'll tell you what, Norton," Josef said, squeezing his tension out into the cloth balled up in his fist. "If you can convince Steve to give up on his silly tea and saucer sets for something simpler, then perhaps we can set up a meeting next week sometime. I'm sick of doing all those dishes for the few bucks we charge for a damn cup of coffee or tea." Josef seemed to be testing out a bit of humor. Norton didn't find it amusing at all.

"Well, you won't be having any of those concerns for very long because I have all the evidence I need to have this repugnant hole closed down," Norton said.

Josef chuckled. "Are you drunk?" he asked, clearly ignoring the threat as if Norton was joking too.

"That's none of your damn business! I know you're cooking with contraband," Norton continued, "and I'm not going to wait for one of these people to die while I am in charge of this district! If you were a real cook, you would be able to impress without cheating and stealing these people's money."

This seemed to have a greater effect on Josef, and he focused his eyes on Norton's. He began whispering through his teeth slowly and just loud enough for Norton to hear.

"*You* make *me* sick, you leech, you sick little leech-man. It's *your* kind that has given me the edge, and you are too damn stupid to even realize it," Josef seethed.

Norton remained speechless a few silent, uncomfortable seconds as he attempted to meet Josef eye to eye but kept drifting away.

Finally Norton slammed his greasy palm on the bar to break the tension, and it made a heavy smacking sound like a sea creature's flipper on a rock.

"If you were smart, you would just do what is mandated and be able to relax and enjoy yourself. Have some fun like everyone else and not work like a slave while endangering these innocent people!" Norton said this loud enough again for everyone to hear.

Josef had finally reached his breaking point. He pointed his finger inches from Norton's sour ruddy face.

"Your concept of fun causes me more stress than my work does. I don't know what my purpose is. I don't even know if people are to have a purpose of any kind. But I sure as hell know that my purpose isn't to fight against the will I have in me to create. I will not just sit around and pretend to 'enjoy' the things you consider fun. I have tried, and even if I'm a weirdo, at the very least I am smart enough to know that those 'things' don't bring me any joy." Josef lowered his now trembling finger. The rage left his eyes as if he'd had some kind of satisfying realization. He finished his thought. "So instead, I am cooking food. I'm creating my own joy, not buying someone else's." Josef took one more look at Norton, up and down, and with a sideways head-shaking look of pity in his eyes, he turned silently around and walked back toward his work.

Norton could feel the silent gazes of everyone in Cigarette's burning holes all over his body. His neck felt hot and clammy. He felt a lifetime of anger building instantly and overwhelming his whole body. In that instant, he dropped his clipboard on the bar. He grunted, and with all his marginal might, he forced himself from his stoop and followed Josef into his kitchen.

***

William knew Norton very well. Not only did he frequent the precinct to try to force the hand of the law on bylaw violators, but he had loads of traffic violations as well. William had handed him two tickets for speeding and one for failure to stop at a red light. After reviewing his records, a pattern of carelessness became obvious: there were speeding tickets, a hit and run of a pedestrian that Norton insisted was "just a bump," several distracted-driving violations, and one impaired-driving suspension. His demeanor was very different when he came to the cop shop to report "gross violations" than it was when he pleaded to have his own penalties reduced. Martyrdom was a hard sell for Norton.

William felt that the new health regulations were infringing on business owners' basic freedoms. The decisions had been made with deep political implications and a huge potential for corporate gains. He tried not to get involved, but Norton seemed to be treading dangerously close to the edge of full-blown harassment lately. More importantly, right now, he was interrupting a night with Cynthia that was supposed to be relaxing. One signal

from Steven or Josef, and William would have to spring into action

and remove Norton from everyone's peripherals. He secretly

wished that such a situation was about to transpire.

William and Cynthia made believe that their romantic night

out wasn't being interrupted by the squabbling near the cash

register. They diddled with their touch tables and played a colorful

game that consisted of flicking balloons at your opponent while

they tried to pop them all by flicking tiny fireballs at them. Cynthia

was letting William do a bit better than he should have been, but

was still ensuring a win each game as per usual.

At the end of one of the rounds, William flung his last

fireball and missed a big grouping of balloons that Cynthia had

gathered. "Damn! So close," he said, not really caring about the

loss but more excited about the closeness of his shot. He was

getting better, but Cynthia always left him something to strive for.

"You may have got that one if you weren't so distracted, my

dear," Cynthia said, referring to the situation with Norton and teasing William about his wandering attention span, which was a point of contention.

"I know. It still frustrates me that someone like Norton is in a position of power, though, you know? God, I hope he doesn't have any little rodent children to perpetuate his cycle of idiocy." William spat out the words "rodent children" like you would spit out a hair.

"Relax, Will," Cynthia said calmly. "Plus, who knows what his kids would be like? Ours turned out waaay different from us."

A mixture of pride and disbelief crossed William's mind when Cynthia mentioned their now grown children. One was an Internet based lawyer, which William had trouble coming to terms with at first. The other was, well, whatever she wanted to be for any six-month period of time. Not to say that she was a disappointment, however. Everyone who met Maye adored her, and she left a trail of broken hearts at each place of employment and in every country she left.

"That's very true, but still they're both good kids," William confirmed.

"They are. We are lucky." William reached out his left hand and Cynthia grabbed it, squinting her eyes with a smile. He cherished this quiet moment, his date with the woman he could not possibly have loved any more. The mother of their wonderful children, his best friend, the passionate, sensitive, goddess-like figure of his fantasies. Their date was going well, and their undoubtedly terrific food hadn't even been ordered yet.

When Norton and William's squabble at the bar became audible, William tensed and began to stand up just as Cynthia rested her hand on his. She shook her head. William settled back into his seat obediently for the time being. After a moment he could see Steven approaching carefully with a tea set on a tray.

"Ahh, perfect, our tea's coming." William said. Cynthia turned to have a peek instinctively. William noticed that she was distracted and flicked a few balloons up on the table screen to try to get a head start on the next game. Cynthia turned around quickly.

"You little bugger!" she said and started returning fireballs with surgical accuracy.

Chapter 17, Loving Grasp

Cynthia was a work and play at home housewife. She spent the vast majority of her adult life no more than a block away from her home. She enjoyed the comforts of living this way and didn't care what anyone thought about her lack of enthusiasm for elsewhere. She and William had purchased their place when Cynthia was halfway through her first pregnancy. The house had three bedrooms, which she had thought was more than they needed, but William had big plans. While they were making their purchase decision, William had said, "I think this guy's little sister is going to want her own room!" as he rubbed Cynthia's growing belly. She had thought it an extremely presumptuous thing to say at the time, but as it turned out they did have another child. When they were a four-person family there seemed to be *just* enough room for them all to coexist peacefully.

They ended up growing quite comfortable and kept their home even after both their son and daughter had moved out. Cynthia decided to make her room into an office so that she could leave her job and start her own business. She proved to be a very talented web designer and marketed herself and her skills like a professional. With the extra income coming in, in addition to William's salary, and the kids now grown and taking care of themselves, Cynthia spent some money each month on improving her computer room. In less than a year, the office had been fully converted into an entire alternate reality, gaming, work, and learning center. Cynthia's kingdom of knowledge and exploration was her sanctuary, and whenever William was at work, night or day, she would be within her boundless cube exploring ideas, other countries, the cosmos, or simply fine-tuning her reactions and coordination skills. Her skills surpassed her motivation, however, and eventually she quit her web designing to pursue her version of retirement, most of which took place in her computer room.

Even in a world so dependently leashed to devices, many of the people Cynthia knew still considered her indoor lifestyle habits strange. They couldn't believe that she wasn't taking beach vacations or buying flashy things. This judgment didn't bother her, since she was happy, and her closest friends and family usually supported her. Cynthia's friends were the second most important part of her life after her dear husband, and she cherished her limited and intense relationships with them. She made efforts to see them periodically, but it was usually at her house or in nearby coffee shops, which was aggravating for those always having to come see her. She was on the receiving end of a lot of invitations, but something more important often seemed to come up.

When she did meet up with someone, she found herself listening much more than speaking, and since her friends loved to talk this suited everyone well. She didn't believe that a person needed to talk in order to participate in a conversation, and she noted that most of her reactions were nonverbal in situations where people were searching for her input. A few headshakes of disapproval, a smile of enjoyment, perhaps a "Hmmm…" to show sympathy for a difficult problem. It was delightful to listen to her friends and be silent. It was at these moments that she finally realized the attachment to the earth that she so desired; when she had to speak she was once again lost in her considerations.

The convenience of electronic communication had created a world increasingly populated by the socially inept, but Cynthia was not an example of this. For many people, years of being cloistered in the safety of their homes and hiding behind monikers did tend to worsen their general disposition and their ability to cope with human contact. She was interested in this subject and had written several blogs outlining some of the disorders created by electronic devices of every kind. Even though she was her own guinea pig in terms of chosen isolation and the social consequences, she believed there was more opportunity than threat offered by a lifetime spent online—if it was approached correctly. Her thousands of followers agreed with her.

A common assertion was that people were evolving a decreasing need to interact. Contrary to this belief, Cynthia wrote that effective living, working, and playing in a world overburdened by information required an even greater ability to communicate, even if this was electronically or indirectly achieved. Akin to how the cavemen needed only a basic variety of grunts to alert one another to danger, or to impress the more attractive of the cave hags, the necessity for good verbal communication was not as vital, because there was so much less noise. Now there were so many avenues to connect with another individual on personal, creative, professional, and recreational levels that combating the increasing volume of unwanted stimuli required constant effort.

Communication was so important for personal development, but who said it needed to be face-to-face, or mouth-to-ear? Even if the parameters of the conversation were fuzzy, even if the dialects were different, or the opinions were contradictory, just to feel that the other person was vibrating on the same frequency as you was transcendent. To Cynthia, it was even a spiritual and undeniably important experience. There were few things more exhilarating than the spontaneous excitement that arose when someone else cut through all the nonsense and still agreed with your ideas. That was what people were searching for in online forums.

So much negativity could be seen online as a reflection of people's need to vent, their immaturity, their ignorance, and their frustration with their own inability to express themselves. Those truly looking to explore, infer, debate, and learn, however, knew better than to stifle this opportunity with threats or sarcasm. Those conducting themselves on a higher level challenged themselves to explore their true innermost thoughts and feelings. This wasn't only thrilling when the user was deemed correct, but it was also thrilling to simply stop the spin of disillusionment on either side of the conversation and end a paragraph in the perfect silence of truth.

Even with all her love for humanity and its advancement, especially in the realm of technology, Cynthia admitted and faced the startling realities of her generation head-on. The general incompetence and immaturity grown out of the very classrooms she attended was saddening. So many people were raised on instant gratification and a skewed sense of priorities, with no real thirst for truth, no real desire to live life. Just ego-driven, smug, self-satisfied facades covering the hollow shell of a being who never created or did anything. Never experienced anything significant and never grew. They were Fabergé shells of polluted eggs—sad, unfertilized souls unable to blossom.

Every emotion and desire had a way of being artificially satisfied. Love notwithstanding, one of the saddest ways to get electronically filled up was pseudo-accomplishment. Virtual reality games of this nature produced kids who whined daily after every request to try or to attempt various tasks. Commonly uttered phrases like "Why do *I* need to?" "That's not my responsibility," and "I didn't sign up for this!" were very frustrating to parents, teachers, and employers. This seemed self-contradictory, considering their commitment to engaging in games and e-world endeavors that required extreme time commitments and huge sacrifices. These investments also offered very little if anything in return. Young gamers often felt like the burdens of all their level gaming or status advancements were visibly radiating when in the real world all that was noticeable was their irritability and irrationality. They felt more than entitled, they felt that they needed time off from their own distractions. They were, after all, owed for the saving of the human race again and again.

Cynthia was also interested in those who had been raised by simulation games and were now adults. As any sane person would, these people clearly understood the difference between the games they played and reality. However, they treated people like they treated the avatars in the games. Life was full of cause-and-effect relationships, and people were more of a means to various ends than actual complex sentient beings. There were no two sides to situations, just the player's take on things and nothing else. The greatest losers in these relationships were usually the gamers themselves, though. They struggled so greatly with the unpredictability of their subjects. The unpredictability and

sometimes irrationality of human behavior was so terrifying that it

left more and more frightened, angry, and confused adults stuck

pale and close behind their computer screens.

Safety was hardly the reason Cynthia spent so much time

inside. She had always loved balance, and although she excelled

in every format of electronic amusement and had even

successfully conquered commerce from home, she still loved to

counter some of her good deeds with feeling like a badass. She

liked to drink, mostly with Will and her good friends, but sometimes

alone as well. She spent good money on fine liquors and loved

single malt scotch, clean distilled vodka, and expensive artisan

gin. William knew about her love of drink and often took part in the

buzz and debauchery. He didn't know, however, that her tastes for

thrills existed beyond this. She was also a secret exhibitionist and

took a huge rush from her exploits.

Her computer room was essentially a glass box. There

were no windows, but when the satellite images of outside were coordinated on the screens it made it seem as if there was no room at all. Cynthia would do many things in her glass box partially clothed, with the screens turned to the invisibility function so that she could see the outside world and take in the high of being exposed. It was a little perverse, and knowing this added to the excitement. She got good use out of the sexy outfits William bought her, more than he would ever know. She was also particularly good at not leaving too much of her own scent on Williams clothes prior to him using them. The uniforms draped off her short and curvy figure. She peered through strands of her short, graying hair as she heated herself up, doing her best to look into the eyes of people outside.

Cynthia often encouraged William to use the computer room as well. Occasionally he would do some virtual-scenario police planning or perhaps plot detailed ideas about crime scenes and other ideas he was having at the time. But the room belonged to Cynthia, and he felt exposed in the glowing square when he was alone. It had always impressed him how she had developed such a tool. She had everything. The floor was covered with a clear mat. You could see right through the mat to the heated tile underneath. The four walls and ceiling had been broken into a grid pattern that was only visible when the entire system was powerless. Otherwise, every surface was covered with panels, information grids, placement markers, and every imaginable customization. Since he only knew the basics of operation, it was a very humbling space for him. It was a far cry from being captain of the police force, where everything was under his command.

For a long time, when neither of them was working the room to its potential, Cynthia had set the walls to project breathtaking scenery. Usually it was set to display large windows looking out over a seaside cliff. This was her favorite. After a while she felt like living this way might eventually ruin her grasp on reality. One day she caught herself watching a hurricane disaster on the world news, and the gritty visceral truths of the outside world crashed into her perfect dictator's display case. This caused some major personal conflict about whether she was becoming too detached from actuality, and after writing a few blogs and receiving some suggestions she decided to change the display and try another experiment.

She decided to start using the invisibility function instead of the paradise displays. This made it seem as though her room hadn't any walls at all, and she was looking at whatever was happening out on the surrounding streets in real time. It was never as beautiful and perfect as paradise, but she felt more in tune with William when she saw her own localized real world more often. She began enjoying the invisibility function when she worked out with her virtual coach or when she was researching, reading, and listening to music, saving the paradise for her and her husband to enjoy together at the end of their day, as a treat.

After dinner she would often lure a tired William off his seat and into her entertainment cube. They had both learned to become excellent dancers over the years. They now trained to the rhythmic sound of pitch-perfect music in a room surrounded by dense wet jungles, waterfalls, and seaside cliffs. It was bliss. She suggested briefly that they should dance in the nude, but after one attempt they both understood that very little dancing would get accomplished this way.

***

Cynthia's work had brought her many honors. She was a successful and respected blogger with tens of thousands of followers. She had achieved three separate degrees in her lifetime, all via correspondence; two were bachelors' in social sciences and the other was her master's degree in biology. Many of her papers centered on the development of social habits in an increasingly artificial world. One of her most famous articles was titled, "Exhilaration Is Not a Whore." It was well received in a few intellectual communities. She believed strongly in the pursuit of excitement, pleasure, and gratification, linking the achievement of these desires with personal motivation. It did seem that society had moved past the point of excitement and was becoming more numb from overstimulation. She had a lot of scientific backing, but it didn't take very long until every point became a cause for another argument. Her interest in this eventually fizzled, just as it had in web design. Nothing rivaled the unparalleled importance of asking well-considered questions and listening to the answers, but with so many answers she was growing tired of the concept.

She moved on to an interest in medicine, but after obtaining her master's degree she had rejected the idea of becoming a nurse due to the corruption she had seen in nearby hospitals. She wanted to help people but decided that she needed to find another avenue. One of her nieces happened to mention that she was a DWO one day, when she was visiting her sister. She explained how she did home visits for those needing treatment who couldn't afford it. Cynthia was set up with a secret contact, and after a few meetings over coffee her DWO contact decided he could trust her. He followed her online, had read several of her blogs and was just short of starstruck.

They trained together for months to ensure her skills were adequate, and soon they were. She was introduced to various warehouses and basements with impressive equipment that was shared with other DWOs. There were large units such as a dialysis machine, ultrasound machine, and lots of equipment used for various testing and analysis. There was even an X-ray machine and room located in a retired doctor's reconditioned basement. This equipment was spread out all over the city, and some of the locations were farther than she had been from her home in years.

Most of her job consisted of simple diagnoses and pretreatment, as well as checkups for those with ongoing illnesses. She also administered some black market pharmaceuticals, which was especially controversial due to the potential for abuse. But people needed help and were getting substandard treatment based on their income bracket. The only other time in her life she had felt this much pride in what she was doing was watching her children grow up into good people. She still considered this an even greater, albeit far less recognized, achievement. After a few years practicing, being audited, and going through a great deal of study and secret meetings in after-school-hours classrooms and private basements, she had earned a renegade's degree in medicine.

***

William had gone home after a particularly hard and long night driving through the ghettos. He slept off and on throughout the day, and since Cynthia was home she had lain beside him and worked from her laptop, organizing and reviewing one of her patient's charts. She had to calm Will down twice after he woke up in a fit. The second time he woke up, he had tears running down his cheeks, but after calming down a bit he wiped them off, said he was okay, forced a quick smile, and returned to sleep. Even though he had shrugged it off, Cynthia knew that William didn't feel the need to cry very often, and the image slowed Cynthia's world down. She remembered the few other times this had happened, mostly when William's eagerness had been broken as a young officer. She lay there silently while she watched him sleep and stroked his hair.

He awoke after another twenty minutes or so and saw Cynthia lying on the bed and looking at him, having closed her computer and put it away.

"I thought you were working," he said.

"Oh, shut up, William," she said, smiling as she squeezed him. "Let's get you out of here and have some fun. I can tell you're on the brink."

William was a little confused but then remembered the tears he had felt earlier. "I guess you're right. I'm fine, though. But, yeah. Let's go out and enjoy ourselves, hey?"

"I'm glad you're on board, my dear. I think we both need a bit of a break. Let's get out of bed and get cleaned up."

"Sounds good." William replied dutifully.

"You actually looked good with a few tears," Cynthia teased. "Way cooler than a crying child."

"Ha! Next time I'll try for snot running down my face to bring us back to the good old days," William said.

On that note Cynthia suggested they share a shower. They weren't fully sure whether they emerged from being pressed against the warm and wet tiles dirtier or cleaner than before, but they both felt marvelous regardless. They preened and trimmed themselves and took turns mixing a few drinks to loosen each other up. Cynthia filled up a little flask with her specialty vodka and, with an enormous wink, suggested going to Cigarette's for a few juices.

"You're a dangerous old drunk," William said to Cynthia as he took a swig from the flask without flinching.

"This is true," Cynthia replied, grabbing the flask back for a swig. She coughed as her over-exuberance allowed a tiny amount of the strong liquid down the wrong hole. They both laughed. Cynthia shook it off and tucked the flask into her purse.

"Let's go see what the night has in store for us, Captain."

Chapter 18, Assembly

Josef was more or less silent in concentration. He was taking his time cleaning and repairing a high quality secondary coffee machine that Steven had recently picked up for next to nothing at a yard sale. Steven was leaning on the table across from him, not quite sitting on one of the bar stools but resting gently against the front of it. He talked at Josef who bobbed his head up and down gently, listening to the pop song Aadir had queued at his table. Josef liked that Steven was relaxing for a moment as there was no way to predict how manic any given evening could turn out to be. For the time being there was an enjoyable clubhouse feeling to the whole scenario and it was Josef and Steven's clubhouse.

Steven had just dropped another couple of pints at Kalvin and Jesse's table, and Josef could hear them alternating between arguing and laughter. Aadir and Anna had been doing their best to distract themselves with their devices as they picked away at a huge cinnamon bun and contentedly sipped their coffees. Josef had finished all the prep work he intended to do for the day, and at the moment he and Steven had everything they needed and were enjoying the opportunity to relax publicly. Sharing their contentment with friends and strangers created an aura of a life well-lived.

Josef was listening to Steven without much reaction but was still adequately absorbing the chitchat as he stared at his project. The problem was that some wiring had come loose from its mounting behind several panels of aluminum. Locating the loose wires was the X at the end of a treasure map. He felt like he was contributing to their success at that moment, making something that would increase their revenue from something that might well have been a freebie. He had always gotten off by capitalizing on cost-benefit relationships. This confidence in his abilities made him happy, albeit a tad preachy at times.

He interrupted Steven's story about some strange street person he had encountered on his walk home.

"The only thing that matters is a person's adaptability, Steve," Josef said, while carefully screwing back on some indescribably shaped piece of teal plastic. "It's the ever-changing ability to scale and sort the importance of information." He placed a screw among a few other tiny screws on the bar. "And the ability to act on the best option. And to follow through! You have to have follow-through when you act."

Steven jumped on this. "Generalities can be misleading, my dear. Even though you love them so much. It's *all important*. Everything is. It's important to be concerned, to have humility, to have a sense of humor and balance with all the cut-and-dried stuff you were just talking about too. All of those reasons are *clearly* why we're so successful, you strange devil." Steven chuckled.

"I do love being a man with a range of abilities," Josef said, proudly patting his prize on its recently completed top. Two little screws remained. Josef swept them carelessly into a little tub with a bunch of other similar screws, nuts, bolts, washers, and tiny springs.

Josef expected Steven to have something to say about the remaining parts, but instead he was glancing over at the two tables with customers seated in them. To Josef it didn't look like they needed anything, but apparently Steven wanted to go investigate anyway. Josef grabbed the coffee machine and the bowl of parts and went to put them away in the kitchen.

Right then the front door opened, setting off the gentle chimes placed above the doorjamb to alert Josef and Steven when guests or troublemakers were entering. Cynthia strutted in with William right behind her, as he had been holding the door to facilitate her entry. She was dressed in a soft-looking sweater of several shades of red. It hung on her loosely engulfing most of her body, and her black leggings and boots were lost enough in the garment that it gave the illusion she was hovering. Or perhaps it was the somewhat swaying dancelike motion she exhibited as she entered that completed the effect. She was the embodiment of someone who knew exactly what awaited her in her chosen excursion and was thereby proud in her decisions leading up to that point. Once Cynthia had crossed the threshold, William let the door swing slowly closed behind him.

"Always the gentleman, Sheriff!" Steven set his charm to flatter.

"Always," the sheriff replied pleasantly.

Josef nodded to William and then to Cynthia, with his hands still full. "Good evening," he said, close enough behind them to smell the mix of cologne and alcohol. Cigarette's was a little quiet for a Thursday night, right before what was usually the dinner rush.

"Look who came to party..." he said under his breath, excited at the prospect of some of his favorite people deciding to spend a bit of their time and money with him. William and Cynthia sauntered over to the booth adjacent to the outdoor patio exit.

He noticed that Kalvin in the corner had raised his head out of his beer and had sat up a little straighter after William entered. It was a pleasant and childlike manifestation of respect.

Josef set the coffeemaker down and was working to find a logical place to set the jar of parts away amid all of his cooking tools. Steven returned to the kitchen and reached around Josef to retrieve a serving tray for tea.

The back door was the next to swing open, and instead of chiming bells it swung into the wall as if it had been hit with a club. The dumpy, disheveled vision of Norton the health inspector was a huge contrast with Cynthia's entrance and her aura of effortless beauty. Norton stopped for a split second to stand and stare, huffing a bit before making his way to the counter.

Josef stuffed the spare parts into the cupboard. Norton looked even worse than usual, enough so that Josef didn't initially recognize him. Usually he would be at least pretending to shuffle some papers or organize his clipboard as he waited, but this time he let an empty clipboard drop onto the bar and promptly and loudly cleared some gunk from his throat as if this was a more attractive noise. Josef chose to temporarily ignore the situation.

The service bell rang a couple of times.

"Someone is here to chat," Steven said.

Chapter 19, the Big Reveal

Josef could not believe that Norton had neither picked up on nor reacted to Josef's obvious cues to leave him the hell alone. He pulled a large bowl of colorful vegetables out of the fridge, anticipating its order. When he turned around, Norton was uncomfortably close and breathing heavily enough that Josef was glad for the plastic wrap over the healthy side dish in his arms.

"Looks like one of those fake building inspector medics or whatever, Steve!" Josef yelled out of the kitchen over Norton's shoulder. Josef continued the ruse, and he gestured to Norton. "Care for some salad, Norton? Freshly made … right now, in fact! So fresh that the lettuce damn near screams instead of squeaks when you break it."

"Save the crap, Josef," Norton almost spat through a mouth that seemed to have a serving of syrup still lingering in its recesses. "I'm cutting right to it. I've been monitoring your wastes very carefully, and as you obviously know it doesn't add up. It's

like you're just dumping in half a can of one thing in here and

there, only to maintain appearances, but there are never any

matching plate scrapings."

Josef enjoyed hearing this. "Our customers rarely leave

leftovers, Norton. They eat my food as if it's the elixir of life. Either

that or the last food on earth. And it is. It's both."

He closed two cupboards that had been reorganized to

accommodate the bulky coffeemaker until it was tested.

Norton's frown was uninterrupted by the comedy. "Cut the

nonsense. I'm still finding the odd leftover, but it never matches

the sauce. In other words, you're throwing out approved sauces

and *serving* other sauces for your dishes. I have warned you about

this numerous times, yet you are still noncompliant."

Still riding the high of his triumph over the coffee machine,

Josef continued to block and counter his attacker.

"We feed leftovers to Cerberus after we're closed. Waste

not, want not, and all that, you know. You may be finding some peas in there, however; our crazy dog won't touch them. What a gem! Gem of a good dog."

Norton knocked his fist on the edge of the table with what looked like an involuntary twitch.

"I said cut the crap, Josef," Norton grimaced. "There is an abundance of just … just sauce and wasted ingredients! Soup, gravies, oils and other liquids. You're throwing things out knowing that I have to spoon through it, and I've had enough of it."

Josef finally somewhat acknowledged this accusation. "*Maybe I'm just sloppy,*" replied Josef, hissing the words out slowly.

"Well, at least we can agree on something," Norton replied.

Josef's anger was building. He pushed past Norton and set the bowl on the counter so that he could open the door to his walk-in freezer. He glanced around and located a large jar of "ranch flavored" dressing.

"Look at this garbage, Norton," Josef exclaimed when he returned. He unscrewed the cap and shoved the jar of yellowish gunk toward Norton. "You're the inspector. Tell me what it looks like."

Norton replied quickly, "That looks like salad dressing. And it is certainly not whatever you are thinking about serving here tonight in that bowl over there." He pointed at the salad that was ready to be served. It clearly was bathed in a different creamy sauce than the yellowish ranch-dressing tub. It had a light pink color and poppy seeds.

"The tub looks like baby shit!" snapped Josef. "I bet it tastes the same way too, but I would never know." He screwed the lid back on and began to walk away.

"Exactly!" fired back Norton, causing Josef to slow his steps as he walked back towards the ranch dressings resting spot. "Because you have never tried it. You have never served it, and you are a common criminal."

Josef turned around and met Norton's cloudy, squinting eyes. He had intended to return the jar to the walk-in cooler, but plans had changed. He didn't break Norton's gaze as he walked toward the prep area while unscrewing the jar's lid again. His steps were intentionally loud and this effect caused Norton to recoil defensively. He moved toward the trash can perfectly in Norton's view and turned the jar upside down, dumping the thick liquid into it. It bubbled out and made little splattering sounds as it landed on top of its own bulk.

"You don't know what I can do to you, Josef!" Norton threatened.

Josef was unshaken. He let the nearly empty jar fall from his hand into the bin, still without breaking his cold stare at Norton's face. It hit something in the trash hard enough that everyone within earshot could hear the glass pop. There was enough adrenaline in him that the shattering glass didn't even garner a flinch. He looked into the trash can.

"Enjoy digging through that, Norton. Really enjoy it."

Josef used to dump any of his monthly sauce prescriptions that were past the point of saving with spices, herbs, water, and vegetables straight down the sink. After catching Norton digging through the garbage, however, his technique had changed. Over the last few months, Josef had in fact been adding a great deal of various unpleasant liquids and solids directly into the bins before taking them to the curb. This included Cerberus's poo-bags and, one time, a good full bladder's worth of Josef's own urine. He liked the thought of this contemptuous action reaching its intended audience. It was a great success.

Thankfully for Josef, Norton had no way of stopping someone wasting food. There were authorities to stop almost every other form of waste, but so far you couldn't force a restaurant to use its food any more than you could force a person to eat. Norton would likely have changed these oversights if he could. As long as Josef continued to buy a reasonable amount of approved products to sell, and as long as he sold his food in a clean facility, there was actually little anyone could do to change that. Norton kept failing to prove that Cigarette's had a black market menu, and now that he was known to Josef and Steven on a personal level, the likelihood of proving such a crime without help had diminished almost to zero. Norton had been reduced to nearly the level of a coconspirator, and Josef hoped this was tormenting him.

"Goddamn it, Josef!" Norton began to raise his voice. "Just use the regular sauces like everyone else! There are dozens to choose from. You can have any flavor you want, and all these people can be kept safe!"

This outburst was loud enough to catch the attention of everyone in Cigarette's. Steven cringed near the back booth as he began walking back with William and Cynthia's drink order. Norton was looking for some semblance of reverence. He was always slightly hunched, always leaning on something for support, and today Josef could hear the countertop creak under his unrestrained weight. Norton's limbs were elastic and gelatinous. Balance for him was like a foreign language badly dubbed over.

Any feeling in Josef's voice that had resembled enjoyment, even if it was patronizing, was now pushed aside. He replied in a louder and lower register than before, but it was quiet enough that anyone outside the kitchen could only hear a dull roar.

"Oh, but of course I use only government-approved food products, Norton. Why, it's against the law to do otherwise. Everyone here *loves* the taste of refined sugars, salts, mutant-glutens, nitrates, preservatives, and *baby shit in their mouths*!" His temper was reeling, and his control was running away, terrified of its own future. "Your god's genetically modified seeds are killing people! I'm not killing people!"

Norton looked frightened. "My *god's*? What the hell are you—?"

Josef's mouth was not shut easily with rhetorical questions at this point, however, and he interrupted Norton's stream of consciousness without hesitation.

"Have you ever eaten a real meal? Have you even had food that wasn't flavorless mud or so processed that your body becomes lethargic as it rejects its fuel? Food that is made with love! I am the only person to handle any of my meals before they reach the table, and I know every damn ingredient in every dish! I am the god of my food. You are nothing."

"Well, I don't even care about whatever the hell you are talking about, and I don't trust your hack wannabe-chef judgment!" Norton began shouting louder. "I order you to never make your own food again, or I will personally end your days of cooking forever! It will be the best day of my life on this lousy job dealing with evil, ridiculous people like you."

"Well, geez Louise!" responded Josef, loving the opportunity to patronize Norton fully, now that he had also lost his temper. "Doing something begrudgingly is really synonymous with doing it poorly, don't you think? And I do neither of those things. Meeting a leech like you has only given me even more confidence in my work than I have ever had before."

Norton had a sweaty stain growing on his chest and his body was sticking to the synthetic material in his cheap collared shirt. "I save lives," he said, shaking slightly. A mist of spittle accompanied the hard sounds of his words.

Josef nearly laughed, but his anger had stuffed the comedy of Norton's response down into an inaccessible place. "Like hell you do," he replied, inching closer to intimidate his opponent. "You are a pawn enforcing corporate reasoning that you haven't the slightest idea of." He grabbed a rag that covered his left hand and wrung it, strangling a few drops of water out onto the floor. "You literally do nothing." Josef's tone was passive but his blood boiled on. He was taking joy in belittling Norton. Norton's mouth popped open as if to speak but instead only accomplished showing its hideous interior.

Josef shoved more of his feelings down the opening. "So just *do nothing* and collect your check, leech. But stop looking to others to give you a sense of importance. You have done *nothing*. You have earned nothing. You are just another person who always wanted a title but never had the ability or desire to do anything."

Josef reached onto the shelf and struggled to grapple a very large jar holding something that resembled brown soup. He slammed it on the table and began trying to screw the lid off intending to pour some of this either down the sink or into the already soupy trash can.

Norton began shaking, seemingly aware of Josef's intentions.

"Stop that right now!" Norton yelled out. He pushed back from the counter and rounded the corner to grab the chef. Somehow his movements were faster than Josef expected. He was going to try to control the situation any way he could, and perhaps for the first time in his life he was choosing force as his means. "Put the jar down!" he yelled, struggling with the object and leaning against Josef's force. He could barely get the words out under his wheezing breath.

"No! Get the hell off me!" Josef replied, already growing stifled from Norton's hot flesh seemingly surrounding his torso.

In their struggle the bowl of salad was knocked off the counter and hit the floor with a long, ringing *panggggg*. Josef could hear the sound of footsteps running toward the kitchen. Steven rounded the corner to see the two men hug-fighting the large glass jar.

"Goddammit, someone is going to get hurt!" Steven yelled.

"You're going to get hurt if you don't let go of me ... and let me smash ... this jar..." Josef said to Norton as he struggled.

"Let it go ... you ... piece of shit," Norton managed to say between sloppy breaths.

Steven was right behind them and shouted, "Stop it!"

It had no effect.

Josef saw in his peripheral vision that Aadir and Kalvin were also at the door, silently debating whether the situation was serious enough to intervene. He wondered for a second why Sheriff Will hadn't come yet and then suddenly, as if melted butter had lubricated the whole situation, both men began losing their grip on each other and on the jar. Norton mustered up every repressed athletic desire he had and yanked the jar hard upward and out of Josef's grip.

***

The first sound was a great long tear of Velcro.

***

This was followed by Josef's detached arm spinning through the air twice. It went up spinning above Norton's shoulders, spun a little more than one more full rotation, and landed on the ground without much of a bounce. The prosthetic arm hit the ground and its nakedness became apparent.

***

The second sound was a *thud*, just like any other prosthetic arm in the world would make. The difference in appearance, however, was immediate. As it hit the floor, a puff of green powder blew into the air out of a tiny jar and it gently settled on the floor. Another small jar, previously within the arm's long lid-like section, which had popped off, scattered red power in the direction of Steven's feet.

***

The third sound was the shattering of the massive jar and the instantaneous rush of its contents sloshing out into the corners of the kick plate under the sink.

***

Then Aadir made a bit of an uncharacteristic gasping sound, like a child seeing his first scary movie.

Norton bent down slowly, fixed on the arm now at his feet. No one spoke. It looked kind of like blood was coming out from the end of two of the arm's fingers, which was of course impossible. Even as Norton squeezed the ends of the rubber fingertips making little spurts of hot sauce squirt onto the salad now strewn about the ground, Josef remained stationary. He felt as if the floor had broken beneath his feet, and he was falling into a helpless void.

Norton broke the silence with a callous grin as he shouted at Josef's stunned face.

"I got you!"

Josef looked at Norton's jack-o'-lantern head dripping with sweat and hatred, temporarily ignoring his contorted arm that was residing on the ground.

Norton repeated himself. "I got you. I got you, *you fucking slob.*" He laid each word out carefully so it could resonate. Then he began to laugh. Everyone else was silent, and the hard sounds of laughter hit every part of the room before dying out on the floor. Steven's face was completely buried in his hands. His eyes were invisible, as were the tears making pools in his palms.

Josef addressed the situation and attempted to explain himself. "Look, Norton. We clean each jar and bag every time they are empty. We even bleach the hoses every night to prevent any back-way contamination. It's only—"

"Shut up!" Norton said, jerking his finger close to Josef's face. "This is the most disgusting, dangerous display of negligence I have ever seen."

He kicked the large prosthetic arm on the ground toward the crowd of people who had formed behind them. Everyone seated in the restaurant had now appeared at the kitchen's entranceway. They could see the colorful array of spices in the arm's cavities as it shimmied around the floor, coming to a stop at Anna's feet. Josef's sleeve hung limp and looked as awkward and unexpected as the scene unfolding inside the once lovely atmosphere of the restaurant. A peppy song was still playing on the speakers and continued on sharply contrasting the mood.

"How many sick people have you poisoned over your lifetime, Josef?" Norton spat.

"Oh, for Chrissakes, Norton! You know that's not the case," Steven replied, his face nearly as wet as the floor.

Norton didn't care to be interrupted anymore. "No! You don't know shit! Neither of you know shit." He pointed again at Josef with the hooked index finger of his wide fist. "You can't control this now. And you"—he pointed now at Steven, drawing out the moment uncomfortably—"you are a monster, just like this freak." Steven had his teeth gritted together, perhaps to keep any more tears from coming and further staining his cheeks. "You are both going to spend the rest of your lives in tiny, separate cells. It is now my duty, and with so much pleasure, I permanently shut these doors. This place is condemned. It is fucking forgotten history."

Josef couldn't bear to see Steven so upset. "Norton, don't do this. Whatever it takes, I'll cook with one arm ... I'll—"

"Shut up! We're done here. Now clean up this mess." Norton shuffled and picked his feet up, trying to avoid some of the salad and soup on the floor.

Cerberus must have heard the ruckus and had gotten scared. He came weaving through the people who were blocking

Norton's escape back to the street. His steps made a little pattern on the hard floor: *click, click, click ... click, click, click ...* The dog was shaking, and his tail stiffened and hooked back tight to his legs. He trotted past the people slowly and quickened his pace into a hop as he skipped toward Steven.

Norton gave Cerberus a kick, and the dog fell into the ruined food on the ground. He tried to get up but slipped due to his lack of an appendage.

Josef vaguely heard the sound of someone shouting, "No, Josef!" as he charged at Norton, throwing his weight forward and pushing him with all the force available to him in his remaining arm.

Chapter 20, Mistakes

A lifetime of quick life-and-death judgments had given Sheriff William admirably quick reactions, and even after a half-dozen drinks he still managed to jump in and keep Josef on his feet before he hit the floor. Alternatively, the entirety of Josef's shoving force seemed to be increased exponentially by Norton's girth, and he hit the floor so tremendously hard that the glassware hanging in the bar threatened to break. The sound wave and tremor caused by Norton's fall brought a gasp from the onlookers. There was a second and louder yelp from Cynthia when she saw what Norton had fallen onto.

Norton did not take to the pain of the broken glass embedding itself in his delicate skin and uneven fat very well. He shrieked loudly, in a horrifyingly high pitch and then began convulsing and flipping about uncontrollably in the soup, glass, and lettuce like the twitching half of a bisected worm. This was too much of a commotion for Cerberus, who had managed to get to his feet and who wisely fled the room.

Most of Cigarette's occupants shrunk back amid the confusion and terror. It had all spun out of control so quickly. Cynthia was the only one who chose to act immediately. She pushed through Kalvin and Jesse and carefully waded through the mess on the floor to reach Norton without hurting herself in the process. Cynthia tried unsuccessfully to steady Norton, who was still squirming around and screaming even louder.

William let go of Josef upon seeing his wife putting herself in harm's way. He reached down and grabbed Norton firmly as one might hold on to a child having a tantrum.

"Alright Norton, slow down now," William said.

He continued to writhe about with shocking intensity. Cynthia must have realized that she wasn't helping much and stood back up. William hoped the injured lunatic would do the same fairly soon.

"My God! Stop, Norton!" screamed Cynthia. "You're going to slice yourself to pieces. Please give me your hand!"

This offering of help was at least enough to snap Norton back into his present reality. He stopped resisting William's grasp and cautiously William stood up and checked himself quickly for cuts. It appeared he was fine. He reached out his hands alongside Cynthia to help Norton off the ground.

"Careful, Norton, you're full of glass," William said, his face a mixture of concern and bewilderment.

Norton rolled onto his knees, breathing rapidly and staring at the pool of soup, glass, and now the little drops of blood. William rested his hand gently on Norton's back, like the first touch of an unfamiliar creature. He reached out his hand, this time almost touching Norton's and gestured for Norton to take it.

Cynthia followed suit. "Norton—"

"Don't you fucking touch me!" was Norton's response to the assistance, as he swatted away William's arm.

"Come on, Norton, let's get you to a hospital and get you fixed up now," William said in a fatherly tone.

Norton looked toward William. For an instant it looked like he was considering the help. It also looked like he might cry. It seemed to William that he had taken the bulk of the glass in his chest and neck. There was enough blood that it was difficult to see the injuries. Norton's clear difficulty breathing suggested that he might have even punctured one of his lungs. William could not be certain of this without more examination, since his breathlessness could also be attributed to his physical shape or lack thereof. It would not have been the glass that had cut into his respiratory system, but instead it would have been his girth that had likely broken some of his ribs and his own bones that could have made a mess internally. Norton's hand moved from his wounded neck and face to the ground and back again, unsure of what to do and unwilling to settle. He seemed confused.

William tried coaxing Norton again.

"Relax, Norton. Okay? We can help you and get you to a hospital. Now let's go."

Cynthia bent down again, looking closer at Norton's wounds.

"We need to make sure there isn't any glass left in your cuts, Norton; then I will stitch you up. Just try not to move, okay?" she said.

Cynthia pulled out a small folding medical kit from her purse. William was not happy to see this. Although her heart was in the right place, this could end up getting them in trouble down the road.

"Let's just get him to a hospital Cynthia…" William suggested, hoping she would reconsider.

Cynthia carried on and pulled out an orange cylindrical container half filled with blue tablets. *Sedatives*, William thought, *that's a good start.*

Cynthia spoke softly to Norton. "Here, take two of these painkillers, and try to stay calm. Then we will get you right out of here and clean you up. Can someone get him some water?"

"I'll get a glass." Anna jumped on the opportunity to make herself useful.

William was unhappy with Cynthia's efforts. Was it obvious to anyone other than himself that she might have a few too many medical supplies at the ready? "Cynthia, put those back, please. He may be allergic or in need of something else…"

Norton looked startled for a second again, his panicked breathing even more rapid, then his legs squirmed beneath him and pushed him a few paces across the floor until he was leaning against a cupboard. A look of sheer horror now dripped from his face, more pronounced than his own blood. His retreat made him resemble a cornered insect.

"My God!" he screamed, his voice cracking and wet at the same instant. "I knew it! Everyone in this place is a bloody criminal! You're one of those DWO medical wannabes, aren't you?"

Cynthia pulled back in fear and instinctively packed the medical supplies back in her bag.

Norton then turned his intention to William, and his brow exuded his pure hatred. "And you! You evil fuck!" Norton pointed to William with a quivering spear of an arm. "You know all about her. I am going to watch you all fry! All of you!"

Shakily he unclipped his cell phone from its holster on his belt, presumably to call for help. William watched silently for a moment as Norton mashed at the screen, which soon became covered in fluids. It had clearly shattered under his weight during his fall.

"Norton, stop this. My car is at home, but if you let me drive your car we can get you some help as soon as possible," William said.

"Shut the fuck up!" Norton screamed, and began getting to his feet while holding a growing bloody stain on his shirt below his breast. He seemed strangely pleased with himself now. "I have been waiting for this moment my whole life. I get to rid the world of an entire nest of vermin all at once. My pain now is nothing compared to the pain and fear you will have to endure for the rest of your useless lives. All of you! You're all done living your sneaking fucking lives and you'll pay for your stupidity, you stupid fucks! And my life will be complete!"

Norton spun around with both arms crossed and pressed to his side, as if he was keeping his insides from spilling out. The blood was beginning to build up and very little of his once-white dress shirt remained unspoiled.

"And it's all of you!" He looked back at Sheriff William and spewed words into his face close enough that he could feel and smell his breath. William stood his ground in silence, unsure of what to do. "How can any sheriff let a shit hole like this exist when you know they are breaking the law?"

William regained his composure; he had dealt with insubordinate people who needed help before and knew that eventually they ran out of steam. "Are you done now, Norton? Let's get going. We'll deal with the rest of this mess later."

Norton smiled the smile of a poacher.

"No, I'm not done! And I would rather die than let any of you idiots try to redeem yourself by helping me. This is all your fault! And I'm coming after every one of you who have supported this place. Even you, *Aaaadir*!" He drew the "A" sound out long and hard. "I know you keep that senile old man locked up in a cage in his own apartment, and I know a lot of people in the public sector would love to check in on you. I can't wait to see all the money you've been stealing from him go to some place where it could actually help a few miserable old bastards like him."

Norton's diatribe continued, and at this point he seemed ready to make his next move. He kept talking like he was going to finish a sentence triumphantly then leave but failed to take the necessary first step. He favored pivoting, yelling, and wavering as he bled more.

Norton went on attacking the people around him who were intermittently trying to help him. "And you … the addict…" He pointed at Kalvin before suddenly stopping what would have been another reprehensible sentence midway through its own embarrassment.

"What is that?" Norton asked, his tiny black eyes opening as wide as the flesh surrounding them would allow. It appeared to William that Norton was finally losing his mind. Everyone present stood frozen in puzzlement.

William could see Norton staring at the puddle of food-goo that was collecting near the counter. It looked as if it was leaking into the floor. Norton stepped toward the edge of the counter in silence with a bit of a limp. A three-foot piece of cleanly cut trim had been dislodged during the altercation.

"I hear dripping," Norton said more quietly than before.

"How could you hear anything over all your shouting?" William said. "You're getting delirious."

Norton ignored this. "There was a drip."

Norton kicked the small board aside easily, and it revealed two shiny steel rings. "What do we have here?" he asked dramatically, as if reciting this line to a camera.

"What's what?" Josef spoke up finally. "If you are going to throw us in jail or go to the hospital or accept our help, do it! Just make a decision!"

"I don't have to do anything, and I'm sure as hell not going anywhere so that you can have time to clean up whatever's below this door!" Norton's lungs made small crackling sounds as he attempted to catch his breath.

His shirt and much of his pants were now heavy, dark, and soaked. The garments swam around his lumpy flesh as he reeled woozily.

"Easy, Norton, you need to come with me, now," William demanded.

Norton repeated himself, quieter now. "I don't have to do anything. But. I choose. To open this."

With that he reached down, pushed his chubby fingers into the rings where the loose piece of trim had been, and yanked.

"Ah!" he exclaimed, wincing in pain from his own movements as he pulled up the rectangular door. The section of the floor came up fairly easily on its hinges, and Norton let the door complete its arc and hit the ground loudly as it came to a stop.

He stood peering down the hole. The kitchen was light enough to illuminate the low space a bit. Norton's face glowed as if he had revealed the ladder to hell. The soupy mixture on the floor began oozing into the space. After a couple seconds it became clear that the cellar was full of racks of prepared foods in storage bins—labeled plastic containers full of spices, sauces, and other edibles, all neatly organized and fresh-looking. Norton leaned over the hole with his knees locked in a climax of anticipation. His eyes widened, and he smiled in a clown-like fashion, larger than it would seem his mouth should ever allow.

"I won't ever have to work aga—"

Then there was the squeaky sound of his feet slipping. This was followed by the sloppy thud of Norton's body being repelled by the concrete below. Immediately after this, the only sounds Norton made were minimal and involuntary.

Chapter 21, the Lows

Sheriff William dove in, attempting to grab Norton as he fell. The effort was something akin to lassoing a meteor. After he hit the floor, he even felt a mild wave of embarrassment because of the hopelessness of his attempt. It felt unprofessional. This feeling was quickly dwarfed by the magnitude of what had happened. For an instant nearly everyone ran in little circles, as if unwinding the kinetic energy they had just been blasted with. Moments later everyone positioned themselves near the hole to decide what to do. Norton lay in a wet heap like a pile of sea trash washed up on shore.

Jesse screamed out, "Oh my God, call someone!" But he failed to reach for his own phone to act.

Cynthia clutched her mouth with both hands, somewhat muting her incomprehensible shrieking.

Josef knelt by the hole in silence, staring at the pile of Norton below.

William knew what the discovery of the crawl space would mean for him, Cynthia, Steven, and Josef. He rested a hand gently on Josef's back as he passed by, quickly climbing down the little ladder. On the concrete below he made a show of assessing Norton's neck and back for spinal injuries. He was unsure if there had been any, but when he checked the man's pulse he felt how faint it was. Norton had lost a lot of blood and now had an obvious massive head trauma. He likely had just a matter of minutes left. William knew he had to act now. So he fabricated a lie.

"We don't have time to get help. Quick, help me lift him out!" He figured that at the very least he could justify his actions later by stating that he assumed they would be able to pull Norton out quickly and conduct CPR on him in a safe place until the ambulance arrived. But he knew better. Even if they were able to pull Norton to the top and get him out of the crawl-space crime scene, the drive to the hospital might afford Josef and Steven the time to clear away the worst of the criminal evidence.

The others went along with William's ploy. In the chaos of impromptu actions, William, Kalvin, and Josef ended up at the bottom of the hole. They all tried to keep their voices calm after noticing that they were yelling at one another and that the excessive noise in the smaller space was counterproductive. They began attempting to push the increasingly bloody lump of wet and limp Norton up the ladder. Their efforts were noble but lacked any kind of result other than exasperated frustration. The others pulled from the top, off and on. Anna searched the kitchen in vain for some kind of rope. Norton kept shifting lifelessly and sliding down again and again.

The groups of pushers and pullers changed, and people shouted ideas back and forth for what seemed like hours. Steven had locked the front door and turned the Open sign to Closed. Before turning the lock, he quickly looked both ways up and down the block outside to see if anyone had noticed the commotion. It appeared as though the community was unfazed, so he returned

inside before anyone noticed his suspicious behavior. He had

never been so happy that business was slow.

William had been checking Norton's pulse occasionally as it

faded to a murmur. Cynthia climbed down into the basement after

Norton had again slipped through the weakening limbs of his

helpers. He hit the ground with a slap, and one of his arms

sounded like a wet towel thrown into a bathtub as it snapped to the

concrete. It had only been a few minutes since Norton's fall.

Cynthia checked Norton's pulse. It had vanished.

"He's gone," Cynthia said simply as she looked up from the

hole with her husband standing beside her.

Everyone had blood and sweat all over their bodies. They

were numb from their unsuccessful efforts. No one said anything.

A strange calm floated in the air, along with the remnants of

Norton's spirit. The fear of death was now abandoned and the

uncertainties of life somehow didn't seem so tragic. Everyone

naturally looked down the hole toward William for guidance on how to proceed, more because he was the largest and most authoritarian person around than because he was a police officer. He was the alpha in this situation and they all desperately needed a guide through the impending anomie.

***

William had a soft heart and valued human life, but between his duties as an officer and his loyalty to his family and friends he was presented with a massive moral dilemma. Legally he was required to call 911 immediately and perform CPR on the incapacitated person until an ambulance arrived. He had already failed both of these requirements. He had effectively performed these actions seventeen times so far in his career and had even received commendations, medals, and promotions for them. One of the people who had received his lifesaving intervention, Kalvin, was right there, in the very same room as he. A room now filled with death. Death that some could contribute to William's negligence.

In the past when life and death situations had presented themselves, William always morphed instantly into a different person—a hero, more or less. He had spent his life erring on the side of more, but this time he certainly felt less. He felt an almost out-of-body experience as he followed through on the bizarre path that his soul was shouting at him to continue with. He knew his work wasn't even close to being over, now that Norton was dead, so he decided to continue acting now and to contemplate later, hopefully over a fine cup of tea. The desire for self-preservation and the preservation of those William loved created the idea of a higher purpose. Beneath his conviction lay very grim realities. Selfish realities. The realities of existence.

William was also aware of another startling secret reality: the crawl space in which this, the most bizarre of dramas, had unfolded still had a small amount of the semiprocessed remains from the man who had eaten Cerberus's leg. They were stored in taped-up wax paper bags in the freezer. The bags looked like they held any other homemade ground meat as they sat there, silently radiating sin. There likely wasn't much of the meat left now, but any amount was so, so very much. After William had ended the life of the man who had killed all those poor elderly women, he had dragged the body into that very crawl space. At the time this situation had presented him with the greatest moral dilemma of his life. Norton's recent passing now trivialized the enormity of even that incredible experience.

William felt badly after he killed the "octogenarian axer." He realized that he had let himself be blinded by his own disgust and that perhaps the sicko had been abused by his own grandmother or had experienced some other socio-psychotic nightmare leading to such violent behavior. He knew what the system did to people like the dead man, though. He would have probably ended up preferring a quick death opposed to his fate in confinement. It wasn't the fact that William had taken the life of another man that upset him, but it was more the fact that he had lost control. Not allowing his emotions to contribute to his actions was something he had always prided himself on. It had made him an effective law enforcer and had even helped him with raising his children.

Maybe it was a reflection of his age, but he felt like he had crossed a line right then that had made him cumbersome. Previously, he'd always counted on his cool decision-making, but now he wasn't sure if he could be trusted to match his actions to his own expectations. William had wondered how God would judge one person who had killed another.

He wished that the psycho hadn't run. He'd been so whacked on drugs that he'd almost leaped across the entire room when he finally realized he was being apprehended. His skin hung off his bones and made him slick as a bar of soap. William wrestled to get ahold of him, all the while terrified of getting bitten or scratched and exposing himself to HIV or various other awful blood-transfused diseases. So William began to choke the man from behind. The man thrashed about with unbelievable strength. William continued to bear down on his throat and didn't stop. Even when the body turned into a corpse. He squeezed more, and he himself began gasping for air through the screen of his clenched teeth. Then he let the man fall to the floor.

Now there was another dead man on the floor before him. To William, the math of the current situation had become obvious. No one could be allowed to tell anyone else about the death of Norton the leech. William would again be required to cover up a situation using all the skills available to him from a lifetime of public service. As for Josef, he would be needing his tools and assistance again immediately.

William considered for an instant how many people ended up going missing these days. Most of these missing people were residents of the streets, but nonetheless they were reported missing by someone who knew them, and most of them were never found. He would have to bank on Norton having few friends or family members. Knowing Norton and the way he spent his time, this wasn't likely to be a problem. What may have posed a problem was any one of the witnesses leaking what had happened. He had to make a convincing argument for silence, and fast. People listened to him in general, but at this moment he was required to command this out-of-control situation.

There was no point in telling everyone to stay away, that there was nothing to see here. Everyone was already gathered around, and those who could bear the horrific sight still couldn't help but stare down the well-lit hole and drink in the unbelievable scene. They stood mute. Josef, Steven, Kalvin, Jesse, Aadir, Anna, and even the wide-eyed Cynthia were all waiting and ready to do anything he asked. What he instead intended to command them to do was nothing.

***

Cynthia had been pressing hard on Norton's neck with the rag from the floor, but she shook her head and finally let go. A small dam of congealed blood let go and oozed out, pooling at Norton's shoulders. William helped Cynthia up the ladder and then looked up from the cellar hole to those above.

"He is done," William stated firmly. He began to climb the short wooden ladder to the surface.

All those present in Cigarette's came together in a way that would have looked to any outsider like the grouping of some draconian cult. When William rose, his light drowned out the luminescence of the others. A fairly crusty looking rag sat on the edge of the prep table against the wall, and William grabbed it to wipe some of the blood off his hands. The little crowd divided as he walked through it. He talked slowly to the pale and haggard people he was addressing.

"We all know who Josef is," William said. Everyone looked at Josef as if obeying an instruction to do so. "We all know him and Steve for exactly who they are. They are good people. If today's events ever come to light, you can be sure that both Josef and Steve will go to prison, likely for the rest of their lives. And there will be nothing I or any of you could do about that. They would not only close this place down and incarcerate them due to their innumerable food infractions, which we *are all so thankful for,* but they would also call into question the safety of this place that many ministries have had a bias against for years. They will crucify our friends because the ministries have needed a scapegoat, and it will have finally presented itself. Realistically, various authorities with more power than me will likely say that someone here murdered Norton, and I will certainly be seen as an accomplice."

William looked at the bloody rag in his bloody hands and discarded it in a garbage can with a look of disbelief on his face.

He continued to speak. "What we must do now is work. Hard. Hard, thoroughly, and as long as it takes to sort ourselves out personally and clean this place flawlessly. Then we all must go our separate ways home and *never* speak of this again. Not even to one another. From this day forward, this *never* happened. It will be exactly like a bad dream that we all forget. This is the only way this can end without more unnecessary suffering. This is no one's fault and none of us deserves any retribution." He paused and then looked everyone in the eye to ensure they were alert. "Am I completely understood?"

Jesse and Kalvin had been standing close to each other in complete silence since Kalvin had crawled out of the hole. The moment of clarity was still blurred by emotions.

"I need to hear each of you say that I am completely understood, or otherwise, *please* ask me any questions you need answered *right now,* because after today *this is an imaginary situation to me.*"

William's request for everyone to disassociate from what they had seen was a difficult one. It was like accepting and rejecting two realities at once. Quantum physics of morality.

William repeated slightly louder, "Am I understood?"

Jesse began to nod and then ran toward the bathroom. The sound of him vomiting just around the corner suggested he hadn't made it very far.

"It's understood, okay? You don't have to worry about us," Kalvin said, his voice wavering like a pubescent boy's. "I'm … I'm going to check on Jesse," he let out weakly, and disappeared around the corner.

"We are solid too," said Aadir, speaking for both of them. Anna nodded and looked directly at William. She finally pushed back some hair that had fallen over her face earlier. Their relationships were all now as connected and delicate as the strands of a spider web. William was as satisfied as he could expect to be.

Josef and Steven didn't need to say anything. Steven went to the sink and began to fill a few large pots with boiling water. Josef pulled out a box from the corner full of other boxes and popped open the top.

"There are eight bottles of bleach here to get us started. Everyone begin cleaning from the counter tops, down to the floor and hit every other surface you come across like your lives depend on it." He pulled out a box of rags from the cupboard and was stopped when he saw Steven arrive with the two rolling mop and bucket sets, clearly taking the lead on the cleaning front.

William was satisfied that everyone would now be kept busy. He glanced at Josef, "Alright Josef, let's go." He gestured to the crawl space and carefully descended below, avoiding stepping on Norton's splayed limbs. Then Josef helped himself down, taking a bit longer than William because of the added balance needed for an amputee without any reason to reattach his prosthetic.

"Can you close the door?" Josef asked.

William reached up and grabbed the handle on the underside of the wooden panel and pulled the door closed. A fair amount of liquids oozed out of the cracks. He avoided the sludge as best he could. He took a deep breath.

Josef took charge. "He is already pretty much bled and ready to hang anyways."

William felt that this was a sheer exaggeration, and if it was meant to be a joke it was beyond too soon. He looked at Norton, who did bear an eerie resemblance to a slaughtered pig. William didn't respond.

Chef Josef continued more on point. "I am an expert at this now so it will not be a problem. You will have to trust me. You will also have to begin bagging, and it will not be pleasant. Let's get this done quickly and think about it as little as possible. It is just meat. Just like any animal."

William knew that Josef's words were meant to be reassuring, but he felt his skin crawl as he realized what they were about to do. Norton wasn't just like any animal. He was a man just like them. He was a disgusting man.

Josef reached into a drawer and pulled out what looked to be a massive carving fork that had been bent ninety degrees near the end. He began screwing the tool into the prosthetic attachment at his shoulder. He then pulled out a leather rolled-up mat which he unfurled, revealing a variety of neatly spaced and shining tools.

"Let's get to work," he said.

William looked into the dim corner and saw the old deep freeze he had sold to Josef and Steven years earlier. He stared at it for lack of better things to stare at while Josef busied himself with cutting. He remembered how he had helped the two restaurateurs lower the freezer into the crawl space and get it in place. They had drunk pitchers of draft beer that night until they were blurry eyed puppets with hazy smiles. William knew that the secrecy of the freezer in the crawl space had always entailed something unlawful that he was attached to, and even this had left the cold burden of guilt with him.

Then had come the murder of the elderly-woman killer, and he was still eventually able to look at the freezer with the confidence that he had done the right thing. And now this. William felt oddly like a cow in the slaughter shoot. The path to ruin was preset. But there was always a way to escape or, at very least, to delay a dreary future. He looked over at Josef, who had donned a rubber glove and goggles and was wasting no time at all. A thought crossed William's mind, *perhaps this is as free as Norton has ever been.* But now William had more time than he could have ever desired to consider his own freedom, as he held open and tied bag, after bag, after bag.

Chapter 22, Spillage

Josef had enjoyed descending into Cigarette's crawl space. It smelled old but pleasant, like a mix of damp earth and a hundred years of doing laundry. Below ground level there was a safe, reassuring silence. When he left the ladder, peered into the dark corners, and closed the hatch above him, the womb effect was complete. He felt free to do what he pleased; this used to include a bit of prep, a little inventory, and general organization. There was even an old chair in the corner, which had occasionally been used for five to fifteen minutes of secretive shut-eye. Nothing Josef accomplished in the crawl space was overly entertaining, but he was able to work and sometimes even relax quietly without being interrupted.

Those feelings of escape and peacefulness were long gone now. Many strange new hybrid feelings had replaced them, however—mostly a cocktail of fear, stress, and anger. Regardless of how the space now made him feel, he still went into it every day, religiously working toward a final release. Today felt a little better, because after counting the bags of meat he realized that there would only be one more week of these paranoid adventures before he could return to simply stacking and rotating his frozen goods to ensure their freshness. Currently there was one freezer filled with equal parts frost and frozen meat, and the freshness of this particular animal was of little concern.

Once this freezer was removed in bleached pieces and incinerated, the greatest remaining risk would once again be confined to perhaps losing his business or other tolerable scenarios such as this. Even the possibility of having their license pulled was far less likely now that Norton was gone. When Norton's remains finally vanished, it would be as if the absence of his orbit would allow the sun to return close enough to burst through the smog once again. But for now, Norton's leftovers posed the greatest risk Josef had ever grappled with. The fat man's burden seemed to know no bounds.

There were so many ways of justifying what had transpired. It wasn't as if they had killed Norton; he was dying. After trying to help as best they could, they'd had no option but to allow him to continue his stubborn, hysterical progress. Josef questioned himself less lately, and fortunately he had William to confer with from time to time, breaking their own rule about not talking about Norton's demise. The conversations proved a healthy way to vent their concerns without having to load the pressures of their fears onto Steven and Cynthia. Every time Josef questioned himself and talked through the scenario with William, he felt much better. To Josef, William seemed more intelligent than he, and if *he* believed they were going to make it, then it seemed probable that they would. Worrying about their secret becoming exposed was therefore much less of a concern than carrying out his daily task of disposal and bleaching. After that, all he could do was continue to live as normally as possible.

When Josef emerged from the crawl space, he felt better. The dull light warmed him through the window as he washed his hands. Where business was concerned, Chef Josef had worried that fewer and fewer people would come back to Cigarette's and, more importantly, that his regulars and his new friends would disappear. He caught himself crying a few times, thinking about being forced out of what would likely be his last job. He feared this scenario even more than he feared the possibility of one of his friends ratting on him and the resulting jail sentence. His fears made him tired. He was drinking more lately to get through tired afternoons and evenings of work. The cumulative effect made him irritable, but alas, the tasks were completed each day, and the final goal was in sight.

Josef preferred not to let Steven see him upset. He could not control others and he accepted that, but he felt as though he could control himself and thereby keep those around him safe. The pressure was crushing him, but he'd been able to handle the load up to this point. The possibility he couldn't bear was that the people he had grown to know and love over his years with Cigarette's would abandon him and Steven, and that they would slowly fade into obscurity. Just thinking about this potential loss was unbearably depressing. Living in fear was no way to live a life that had proven to be so unpredictable and often cut short. So instead of focusing on the fragile and terrifying shell he found himself in, he attempted happiness instead and did his best to share this experience with Steven. Each time he came out of the crawl space with Cerberus's breakfast and dinner, he concentrated on this idea of happiness.

***

People uninvolved in the incident still continued to eat at Cigarette's. Josef and Steven worked hard, and their profits were the best they had been since they'd begun. It wasn't as if they were packed, but there were enough clientele to keep busy, and a few more people were now regulars who enjoyed Josef's talents. Perhaps even more importantly for business was the service. Customers who were used to eating predictable meals left satisfied with slightly higher end slop, but Steven's presence would stick with them even after their stomachs were once again empty. Steven went above and beyond being a conveyor, and with an increasing number of self-service restaurants where customers placed their own order on a device and picked it up themselves when they were prompted, the alternative of being graciously waited on felt luxurious.

Steven was much more than a set of legs for the lazy; he provided entertainment and warmth, and seemed to have boundless energy. He was trying to ensure that money kept coming in and felt successful in contributing to it doing so. He was also doing a fantastic job of keeping Josef busy enough that his thoughts didn't bury him. Such effort and commitment proved very effective. They had even considered hiring someone to help serve, clean tables, and do dishes during the lunch rush. Steven and Josef had recently discussed asking Anna if she would like to work for them. The free meals alone would certainly make it worth her while. The prospect of the trials of a new employee, however, would have to wait until the removal of a freezer from the basement made space for the future to seem possible again.

After such a traumatic, unforgettable, and life-changing event, Steven felt he would never again be free from the depressing, undying gloom of guilt. He felt cursed to spend each day paranoid and sullen, molested by something he had never prepared for. But then time happened.

Only a few weeks later a tipping point back into the light of life and happiness had come to him through music. A song recommended by Aadir not only reminded him of better times, but it also reminded him of future potentials hidden, still waiting to be discovered. He felt encouraged to move on. Perhaps Aadir had recommended the tune because of this. After that it only took a few more pushes to change his perspective. He knew what Josef had to go through in the crawl space, but for Steven it was out of sight and out of mind. Steven spent his exhausted evenings happily creating a few hour-long rotations of uplifting and relatable music for the next day. The music began to lap away at his gloom.

Within two months of the incident, the old regulars were back at their favorite tables with their heads nodding to free audio therapy. Their return was the greatest surprise for both Josef and Steven. The informal reunion brought with it a warm, meditative feeling of recovery. Sheepishly at first, they returned and had quiet meals without saying much. After a few visits the crew acted toward each other as if nothing had ever happened. The success of Cigarette's made everyone more comfortable and hopeful. This gave Steven more energy and allowed him to work even harder. He felt that he needed to be the figurehead and the glue to hold everything together and he was smart enough to know that this would eventually lead him to exhaustion. For now though, there didn't seem to be any other good enough options. He could rest when he was dead.

***

Of the group, only William was truly predisposed to the manner in which time softened all blows, yet it was he who bore the remaining gravity of Norton's death the most. He felt that his controlled presence was needed in the only place outside of his home that he had, at one time, felt free to be himself. He realized the punishment's implications and accepted them bravely. He couldn't just leave. Everyone would panic. Even Josef would panic. So he hung on and faked his way through pacifying conversations. The others who had witnessed Norton's fall made their way back to their routines, and although they never fooled themselves into believing nothing had transpired, they did start believing that there may never be the need to realize the consequences of their actions, or lack thereof.

It was helpful for the people of Cigarette's that Norton was such a notorious, conniving, and irritating individual. When the investigation was launched into his disappearance there were several other restaurant owners under suspicion. William headed up the investigation because of his prior interactions with the missing person. Only three blocks away from Cigarette's, there was a pizza joint owner who had actually had a physical altercation with Norton only a few weeks earlier. Norton had predictably reported this "assault" to the authorities, and a scapegoat was born. At the time the scuffle was dismissed as too minor for action. A new officer had been pleased with himself after he had mediated a meeting with both individuals. Now that Norton had disappeared, however, the tough-looking peppy young pizza entrepreneur was a prime suspect. In fact, Norton had been scheduled to visit the pizza parlor the very same day he disappeared, and since William and his wife had eaten at Cigarette's that evening, it discounted the other potentially prime suspect—Josef—from the possibility of committing the crime. The pizza man and several other inconvenienced innocent people shared in the power of death's aftermath.

Of course, no evidence of foul play was ever found, and several witnesses who had eaten at the pizza place during the day were able to attest to the pizza pusher's preoccupation. No leads into where Norton had gone surfaced during William's investigation. In all of his years on the police force, he'd only ever had a handful of petty thefts and other misdemeanors that had gone unsolved. He had previously conquered every serious case he had encountered, which had led to his celebration as perhaps the best cop his precinct had ever seen. William had been very proud of this reputation, although he had tried to hide the sin of pride like all of his others. He was less proud when he found out that he was just as skilled at being a manipulator as a problem-solver. He pretended to become very frustrated with his inability to find even the most basic leads on Norton's disappearance, and rumors of his failing professionalism began to circle. Even though his plan was going as well as intended, he was still somewhat disappointed in how quickly people had forgotten the triumphs of his past and replaced their admiration of him with hopes of their own promotions. The opportunity for William's retirement gathered heavy as a hailstorm on the horizon of his career.

Sheriff William had seen worse ways to die than Norton's exit. Whenever he considered someone discovering the nature of Norton's disappearance, he shook off the feeling of nervousness that haunted him by remembering how all those present had a stake in keeping quiet. William was pleased with the impromptu speech he had nailed that dark day that seemed so long ago now. He considered the possibility that his words would still be offering comfort to those who were likely reeling from the same traumatic experience he was, but with less experience in witnessing human blood and death.

He was more concerned initially for Cynthia's well-being. Even if his involvement was confirmed, he could always create some elaborate story that, due to his position and his mastery of the art of manipulation, he had silenced Cynthia's many attempts to report the death. She could tell of the "tortured nights of guilt" she had endured in order to conceal the truth. She could cry and tremble in front of a jury and recount the fear of an abusive, powerful husband with something to hide. She could convince them that he had assured her helplessness by saying that no one would ever believe a "simple housewife." William would have secretly loved the irony of her pantomime.

William had made his mind up that, no matter what, he would be Cynthia's martyr. They were both convincing enough actors that they could pull it off. She would be saved. More importantly, though, was the unlikelihood of discovery making this backup plan unnecessary. William and Josef had worked together for days after the incident, carefully disinfecting every possible trace of bodily fluids. It had been a more difficult ordeal than they had first expected, and everywhere they looked they could imagine DNA smeared into microscopic cracks.

Every surface, including the floor, walls, ceiling, the ladder down to the crawl space, and Norton's final resting place on the concrete, needed to be bleached, scrubbed, and then washed clean. Methodically, all the cupboards had their contents removed and bleached or discarded. And finally every bottle on the bar and glass panel had the same treatment. It was complete overkill in terms of any type of forensic probability, but in terms of peace of mind it was barely adequate.

William returned to the crawl space every week and would peer into the deep freeze to confirm the rate of Norton's disposal. It had been nearly six months, and the supply of meat had shrunk to a mere dozen or so pounds. Only a few more weeks of feeding Cerberus and there would be no trace of the horror show at all, and he, the only one to truly understand the gravity of the situation, could be free to actually move on and not just pretend.

For now, he smiled and joked about trivial everyday things with the guests of Cigarette's, reinforcing to everyone without a legal background that: *Yes, it is all over. We are safe. We can move on.* But until he finally unplugged and destroyed that deep freeze, and after even the extra power used for it had been paid for and once again returned into the ether of invisible, unbridled transition, he would remain afraid. He would remain with his mouth dry, drinking pot after pot of calming tea.

***

One night after some guests had left their house and they were both happily drunk, Cynthia had heard William's full confession of the process by which Norton was being disposed of. Their happiness had vanished quickly with his long-winded explanation that ended in William's preconceived idea of self-sacrifice for her benefit should they ever be implicated in Norton's death. She had never experienced such a mixture of emotions. What he was saying to her was so insulting, terrifying, and chivalrous all at the same time that she nearly screamed at him, "Absolutely not!" Instead she just looked him in his sad eyes and said, "Absolutely not."

She was insulted because it made her feel as if she didn't have a say in something that involved them both, and prior to that day anything of even *remote* importance—including cereal choices—had to be agreed on. Often these agreements coincided with her preference but not always. The parent-like protective quality of William's plan put her on a level of dependence that made her uncomfortable. This feeling vanished before the emotions formed into words. She knew that this confession meant only that he feared losing her, and it was actually with the utmost respect for her intelligence and powers of observation that he needed her consultation of his plan, in case she found any holes.

There were no problems with the plan that she could think of, other than the extra power that was needed for the deep freeze. He said it was actually Steven who'd first considered this problem, and together, Steven and Josef had been incredibly conservative, unplugging every appliance when not in use and even giving up watching television in favor of playing cards during the first few months when all three small deep freezes were needed.

Cynthia hated to see William in pain, and ever since Norton's death he had been removed from himself like she had seen off and on over their years together. She was still angry, but her caring outweighed her frustration. She hugged William almost violently and kissed his cheeks several times. His cheeks were wet, as tears flowed silently from the downturned corners of his creased eyelids.

"I'm so sorry, Cynthia," he said, sounding weak and nearly winded.

Cynthia grabbed him gently by the shoulders and moved out of their embrace. She briefly removed one of her hands from his shirt to wipe William's face. William's shoulders were sunken away from his neck. There was a small salty stream that had reached the stubble on his chin and was hung up in its friction, not quite ready to fall.

"Okay, Will. You can be sorry right here and now. I will feel the same thing with you. I am so sorry too. But never again. We are done being sorry. We will live out every moment of the rest of our lives with our heads high and our minds clear enough to conquer anything thrown our way. This will be how this ends."

William saw the honest conviction in her eyes. Then he stood up straighter and wiped the tears from his face with a single downward motion of his massive palm. He flicked his hand like it was soaking, even though it was nearly dry.

William smiled, his voice straight and firm now. "That will be how this ends," he repeated. He leaned down and kissed Cynthia quickly and firmly on the lips as he squeezed her arms.

They hugged and rocked back and forth for a few seconds, like new lovers turning their backs to the rest of the world. They succeeded in never wavering to the world's threatening ugliness again and only opened their eyes to the light and kindness they had been banking together for half a combined century.

Chapter 23, Refuge

Early in the morning after Norton's death, Anna had lit herself a cigarette with trembling fingers. She remembered feeling more exhausted on that walk than she had at any other point of her life. She and Aadir's exhaustion felt like their own sunken eyes: heavy, separate, and solitary. Anna had slowly smoked her dainty cigarette down to the filter, as she had with every cigarette before, but she drew little pleasure and no relief from the experience, which surprised her. Her stomach felt sick, and it turned with the motion of her unenthusiastic plodding. That morning she had thrown her cigarette butt on the ground as she exhaled the last puff of smoke she was to ever have.

The first few weeks after that were slow and cruel. The opportunity, craving, and thirst for a cigarette plagued Anna more on than off, but she grew more and more nauseated the closer she actually got to lighting up. She couldn't figure out why, but her sick stomach seemed like a sign to not indulge. The idea of indulging in anything seemed despicable for a while. She decided that if she could leave smoking behind, then in some way she could also leave behind the tragic nightmare evening at Cigarette's. Anna wasn't interested in improving her body for the sake of vanity but it felt like she had more so much more time now. She needed to find something to do with her spare hours and so she filled the gap with exercise.

Initially, Anna did her yoga with a group of acquaintances she had met at a sweaty, stifling basement studio. After Aadir came with her a couple of times however she stopped going. She tried to convince Aadir that no one would care about his acne-scarred neck and back, but he couldn't bring himself to take his shirt off in public. If he sweated in a shirt and couldn't shower immediately, it would always inflame many of the remaining holes. At first Anna agreed to do her stretching at home out of pity, but she began to enjoy sharing their routines and meditation at Aadir's father house. They pushed each other in a playful fashion, and the results were positive.

Anna, as a small and attractive female who frequented public transit and walked the streets amid reckless derelicts of every sort, had decided to let Aadir teach her some basic self-preservation techniques as well. Much of their stratagem revolved around self-awareness and hazard avoidance. She estimated that for every situation that turned into a physical threat, there were ten others she could avoid by being relaxed and alert. The polar opposite of her relaxation-based yoga regimen was the combat which they learned together. They began to explore every option religiously.

For a lanky unassuming guy, Aadir had incredibly fast reflexes and had perfected a few swift and immobilizing moves that had kept him confidently safe to do as he pleased for many years. Anna was a natural, and they sparred continuously in the cramped quarters of Aadir and his dad's small kitchen. At first Anna scoffed at training in such a cramped place, but it made every alley and street corner seem like a massive playground in comparison. She learned everything he had to teach, and then they explored further ways of disarming larger opponents, as well as opponents with knives and bats. There were some moves that could save you from an individual with a gun at close range, but they essentially knew that they were at anyone's mercy who had them in their sights from a short distance. This didn't bother them. They tried their best never to fear the unpredictable.

It really was all in one's mind, Anna had found. The brain is truly the most powerful organ. It controls an individual's body in a more fine-tuned manner than any machine could ever hope to achieve. It propels desire and action. It is the most sensitive sex organ. With its infinite importance, the brain also scores huge points for remaining such an incredible mystery. She felt like when her mind and body were at their sharpest that she actually floated a few nanometers above the earth on which she walked. She had never felt so good.

Anna's goal when she meditated was to keep her mind tuned and clear like the indispensable tool it was. She desired nothing more than to feel the echo of the balance between razor-sharp awareness and the calm found in the heart of the voyage. It was a feeling as pleasant and natural to both her and Aadir as following a road along the edge of a body of water. They felt invincible from any scenario in which they were offered a chance. They felt as if they had achieved complete control.

It was raining in the early afternoon. Aadir and Anna had been doing yoga and listening to relaxing music after banging around the kitchen during a session of sparring and tripping techniques. After they'd stretched for five minutes, the rain cleared up, the sun began peeking through the clouds, and they felt a little run-down and cooped up by their lifestyle and its commitments.

"I feel healthy enough that I need some Cigarette's," Anna said to Aadir, who was still lying on the floor.

"I've been thinking the exact same thing. I've started to really miss it," he replied. They had nearly finished cooling down from their routine and Aadir sat cross-legged on the floor,

stretching his arms.

Anna got up off the floor after pushing out a fully extended

downward dog and took her shirt off slowly, with her back to Aadir.

She began to walk away down the short hall and undid the

waistband on her loose pants allowing them to fall to the ground.

In only her underwear she felt her body begin to cool down. Her

pace was intentionally slow, and she did her best to sway her tiny

hips, hoping to be noticed.

Aadir noticed.

Anna looked back as she undid her bra, covering her

breasts with one arm like a swimsuit model and saw him transfixed

on her with an uncertain look on his face. She felt a hot rush wash

over her chest and neck and the intensity of this feeling was

amplified by the calmness in her mind.

"Quick shower, first?" Anna asked coyly, as she tossed her

bra onto the floor, rounding the corner into the bathroom.

"One has to be presentable," Aadir answered. She could hear him trip a bit on his pants as he pulled them off trying to catch up to her—all his focus and judgment reduced to nothing in a matter of seconds.

They made love quietly as they always did in order not to disturb Sonny who never ventured outside any longer. After they were finished they used the shower for its more intended purpose and began dressing in the bathroom. Aadir was playing with his phone waiting for Anna to finish dressing when there was a commotion in the hallway.

"Ah!" The person exclaimed with a startled inflection. This was followed instantaneously by the thud of a body hitting the ground and the single word, "Shit!"

Both Anna and Aadir sprung out of the bathroom to assess the situation, ready for a fight if need be.

To their astonishment it was Sonny. He was laying on the ground with both his feet entangled in Anna's lazily discarded bra.

Anna, pulled the garment away quickly and Aadir helped his father stand up.

"Are you alright dad?" Aadir asked.

"I'm so sorry Sonny," Anna added apologetically.

Initially Sonny looked confused and seemed frightened. He then looked at the bra in Anna's hand and it appeared that he had formulated a very good idea of what had transpired. Anna was mortified. Sonny said nothing but scowled at them both in turn. He dusted his pant legs off, shook his head at each of them again and returned to his bedroom closing the door behind him hard.

Anna and Aadir went back to their bedroom with their hearts pounding. They looked at each other and began to snicker. They couldn't help but laugh uncontrollably. The harder they tried to be silent the harder they laughed until they were giggling like kids at a sleepover.

"We need to get out of here." Anna said.

"Oh my god, no kidding," Aadir laughed. "I can't believe my dad's first word in over a year was, 'Shit!' "

Anna burst out laughing again as she pulled on her shoes. They headed out the door and were relieved not to see Sonny emerge from the bedroom again before the left.

In the most ridiculous way this had been the best day Anna had since Norton's demise. The horror of death had shocked her so badly that she felt an uneasy sense of continuous vulnerability. Anna remembered her body had felt like a smear of goo covering her life-sustaining organs that were begging to burst below its surface at any time. This was now replaced with a feeling of well-tuned muscles encased in firm skin with a machinelike readiness. Her pessimism had faded as gradually as her body improved and the results on her efforts had a positive compounding effect.

When they first sat down at Cigarette's Anna could tell that Steven was emotional.

"Hello you two, it's really... it's really great to see you both again." Steven was clearly trying to keep a firm and stoic composure.

Anna shot out of the booth and gave him a firm hug.

"It's great to see you too Steven," she said watching him brush a tear off his face. Aadir got up from his seat and gave Steven a handshake that turned into a hug as well.

"I promised I wouldn't make a big deal if you returned but, thank you for coming." Steven attempted to compose himself. "Ahem, anyways, what can I get for you two?"

"Just a couple teas and whatever the best thing is that you're serving today, for each of us please" Aadir said.

"Well you two just happen to be the best thing I'm serving today," Steven replied cheekily. "But I will be back with your teas followed by our special. Josef is doing burritos with salsa verde today and you are going to love them."

"Sounds fantastic, thank you Steven." Anna replied smiling brightly.

"You're most welcome." Steven concluded and rushed off to the kitchen.

After a great meal, Anna and Aadir hung around late into the evening and relaxed in the booth, as they had done in the past. They were happy and felt a sense of bittersweet closure. They paid their bill but stayed to chat with Josef and Steven long after the other customers were gone. They never once mentioned Norton. On the way out, they yelled a thank-you into the kitchen, where Chef Josef had his backed turned. He turned around, smiled and gave them a salute with what they now knew to be his prosthetic arm.

Anna and Aadir felt healed after that moment. The tragedy gave them a new reason to thrive. It gave them a new reason to squeeze every drop out of the everyday. Once they met the other regulars at Cigarette's, it was even more validating since it seemed like they too were trying to live better. It was unfortunate that seeing their friends reminded them of their past struggles but this feeling passed too. Occasionally they were still concerned when they recalled the traumatic scenario, but this was lost beneath daily annoyances and amid the necessity to carry on.

After the shock wore off, and they had contemplated the inevitability of death, they felt the urgent need to experience life again. Anna and Aadir knew what they had and decided to celebrate their love, even if their lives had become much more bizarre than their fairy-tale ideas had intended. They were very happy together; each was the other's best friend and they wanted to have a party to celebrate their dumb luck.

Aadir and Anna went down to the courthouse dressed in their favorite clothes, which in terms of wedding standards were unacceptable street garb. A few of their close friends bore witness, and afterward they all went out for lunch at Cigarette's. Josef and Steven had put up a "Closed for Wedding Reception" sign. It was a little hastily made, since it was probably the only time it would ever be used. A few people came to the door and turned away in disappointment. Josef ignored them. He had prepared a wide range of appetizers and Steven, although no one asked, baked an elaborate multilevel cake. It was Easter-egg blue, which was not representative of anything, but everyone agreed it was pretty.

After a few hours, Josef apologized and said he had a party reservation and unfortunately couldn't afford to lose the revenue.

The celebrants all embraced in turn and parted ways. Anna and Aadir walked back to Aadir's father's home alone. Something about the flower petal overkill all over the house must have stirred a memory in Aadir's otherwise vacant father. He didn't say anything, but he smiled and sat up on the couch from his usual laying position while Aadir and Anna told him what happened. He opened his mouth as if to speak but returned to smiling instead, and for the first time he touched Anna. He reached up to her, and when she bent down to him he placed his hand on the side of her head and looked into her eyes.

Aadir was incredibly tense. His father then looked at him, removed his hand from Anna's head and reached out to him. When Aadir bent down though, the old man simply relieved Aadir of his glass of champagne and settled back into the couch. Aadir and Anna laughed and pulled up two chairs. They refilled Mr. Manji's glass one more time, and after draining its contents he promptly fell asleep. Aadir and Anna carried him to his bed and tucked him in. They were trying not to laugh as they negotiated the corners with his small, fragile body. Everything seemed so silly, so ridiculous, and so wonderful. They closed Mr. Manji's door and began to kiss immediately when it was latched. They worked their way down the short hallway and through the kitchen, trembling in anticipation as they tore off each other's clothes. They let out only whispers and whimpers in near-silent intensity as they consummated their union on the flower petals covering the tiny home that was only somewhat theirs.

Chapter 24, Weaning

Despite aspirations of grandeur, Jesse was never much of a man of action. He had always assumed he would have no problem accepting someone else's death if he deemed it reasonable. He didn't feel as if one human life was overly significant in the universe. If someone had to die for the common good, then that must be for the best of all things. He had seen so much death on television shows, movies, and web videos, with the professional entertainers working hard to make their scenes as realistic as possible. But when confronted with Norton's demise and his bloody, lifeless body right in front of his eyes, without the distance of a screen, Jesse was confined to his shock for weeks. Lost, sleepless nights, waking up in drenched sheets, punctuated his life.

He never cried, but the opportunity presented itself many times. His tears would rise into his face like mercury in a sunbaked thermometer, making the skin around his eyes and nose seem thin. It felt as though it would be temporarily therapeutic to allow the dam to burst, and if he'd truly believed it would help end his suffering he would have submitted to the urge. But he never did believe in much of anything. His suffering only subsided little by little over time, like a slow-motion tuning fork that had been struck and now slowly wobbled back and forth in a frequency that never wished to return to the median.

The best version of Jesse was a clean, smooth canvas taking on the colors of those he admired around him. He wished that others' impressions on him were more fleeting, a mirror reflection instead, but this was not the case. He needed to find a way to whitewash himself and start again, but at the end of each day he was not willing to make the effort. He knew that his lack of action would end up trapping him and that he would be unable to support his own weight, much less any other kind of beautiful impression he may have once desired.

He would find momentary solace in clichéd posts added by strangers on the numerous social media pages he was a member of. He even printed off a page for his near-empty fridge. It read: "Only those things that you choose to give power have any control over you." It had a picture of an old man appearing to hurl a rock up in the air above his head. Jesse used this as a reminder to think positively and not hurl any rocks of anger and sadness too far over his own head.

Jesse also liked to think that he hated people in general, as if this gave death less power. He would, for a time, blog about his contempt with sentences such as:

"We keep finding more ways to save human lives, while at the same time we are leaning harder with our collective foot on planet earth's neck. All we are doing is ensuring that there will be a lot of people left to watch the apocalypse unfold."

Everything he wrote was hopeless drivel, but to him it was

therapeutic enough to add to the depressing mural on his filthy

fridge.

Comparing himself to so many people even less adequate

than him was such a shortsighted high. For amusement he would

spend a lot of time watching videos of others failing at their own

attempts or making fools out of themselves.

"People are so stupid," he would say out loud, as he hoisted

himself out of his computer chair on his way to bed without having

cleaned up himself or his apartment. He would lie, then, in his

greasy sheets and face dreams of his insecurities before waking

up to his alarm without any desire to leave his bed. In a sense,

there weren't enough dividers in his life. There weren't enough

segments to make each part make sense. The result was a

continuum, a blur of meaningless motion, every effort only further

confusing the situation. The lowest points of his life, between

artificial highs and cosmic collapses, made him feel more like a

rubber ball than a person. An inanimate object propelled between locations without consideration. Jesse was now convinced that life just happened around him and that he had no control over the outcome. The best he could do now was get on a convenient path and coast through to see where he ended up.

Jesse was just another adult-sized child, and it seemed like he had a reason to celebrate his losses. At least he wasn't stupid enough to be dead, so therefore he felt smart. He chose not to look outside of himself, which was tragic because he might have seen someone he wasn't expecting. Perhaps then he could have gained some perspective. Perhaps then his competitive prospects and fortunes would emerge from the dark. Even better still, perhaps he could help another person and know such beauty in his power that this previously unknown joy might become ever more desirable. Instead, Jesse was trapped in the comforts of his misery, and Norton's death only made him hate other people more and feel sorrier for himself.

***

Kalvin was called back to work only two days after he had attempted to quit at the recycling plant. On the official record, they never even documented his attempt to leave and instead noted that he had taken two personal days. Someone or some group of people had started a blaze in one of the bins of colorful shredded 94-Series Plastics, and they needed someone who had dealt with this situation before to save them the time and money necessary to train a replacement. More than anything, they wanted to continue operating at capacity, and Kalvin had historically proved to be essential for capacity. As a Senior Recycling Safety Technician, he was always on the cleanup crew for these messes. The fire had already been extinguished, but the toxic smoldering mess had to be dealt with, and the affected equipment needed to be thoroughly cleaned and assessed before being turned back on line. Begrudgingly he got it done.

It was fairly common for the pro-global-trade demonstrators to find a way to get a bunch of fuel onto a pile of scrap and then to devise a way to ignite it. They had succeeded in doing this using every method from Molotov cocktails to focusing a beam of light through a nearby window. Kalvin wondered what exciting new training all the guards who failed to protect the company's assets would be going through this time. Maybe he would even be asked to create a new manual if the ignition method had been particularly creative. He certainly didn't envy the rookies who worked for him. They would likely have a mandatory weekend training course to suffer through as some condescending administrator methodically insulted their intelligence. He loved getting paid double overtime to be the person to do exactly that.

Once the plant was operating and up to code again, it was back to the highs and lows of daily life for Kalvin. One new scheme that he was pleased to be involved in had developed, however. As per Sheriff William's instructions, he had been incinerating various items periodically. He would sneak them in mixed with his own weekly household recycling, just like he had always done, but instead of sorting the goods he would throw the whole bin into the incinerator. He had also adjusted one of the video cameras in the plant toward the door of the furnace room instead of the furnace so he could burn his whole bin and be able to walk out undetected with an identical-looking new blue box every few days. He was in charge of blue box inventory, so fudging these numbers was easy.

Due to the effect that fire had on evidence, even if his strange behavior was called into question for those few dozen bins he burned within the span of a year, the only thing that could be proven was that he was a bad recycler. This type of environmental infraction he would usually deem a crime indeed, but his priorities had to be temporarily reevaluated. Now the only other thing he had to do was wait for the day when he had to personally dispose of a small deep freeze. The previous week, Sheriff William had said that the day for this was coming, and soon. In the meantime the free beers at Cigarette's gave him something to look forward to and enjoy every week.

Chapter 25, the Replacement

The new health inspector had been very impressed with the bleached cleanliness of Cigarette's, and he even ate there occasionally. "Got to eat somewhere I suppose!" he would repeat, as if it was a joke of some kind. He enjoyed the bland carbon-copy food production served to him with admirable consistency. The only problem he noted on his first few visits was the restaurant's name.

"Why would you name your establishment Cigarette's? It implies such a seedy and unclean nature of what is otherwise a pretty good restaurant."

Steven replied immediately. "Thank you so much; we really try hard!" He said this excitedly, before rubbing his clean brown temples with both hands, implying an ongoing headache. "I hate the stupid name," Steven declared. "I hate its connotation, I hate its link to a shoddy bit of history, and neither Josef nor I have ever even smoked…"

The health inspector liked being agreed with.

Steven continued the charade. "It was only really a matter of logistics, though. To rebrand, remarket, and redo the signage is an expense we cannot bear at the moment. More than *anything* we don't want to sacrifice the quality of our food or the cleanliness of our facility by drawing any more from our meager cash flow."

The health inspector took in a spoonful of his salty orange carrot soup, fully engrossed in the story.

"Times are just tough, you know?" Steven finished with this and forced a look of exasperation.

The health inspector knew very well that local restaurants were closing their doors faster than they could possibly be purchased and reopened. The ones that remained open were in increasingly worse shape as he visited them every few months. To keep his job's validity, he had in fact recommended that a few of them in grotesque condition be closed down until they could meet code. They were practically boarded up the next day.

The new health inspector never enjoyed this part of his job, so he felt that it was a blessing that people still chose to eat at Cigarette's despite its wretched name. He could only attribute its success to the overwhelming congeniality of Steven, even though his partner Josef appeared to serve more or less the same thing as every other dead-end joint trying to stay afloat. What he didn't know was that Cigarette's was actually turning a profit, and that Josef and Steven were comfortable with their level of patronage. Their success was mostly due to a group of repeat customers experiencing flavor and enjoyment that the well-meaning inspector would never know.

He asked Steven, "What would you change the name to if, God willing, one day you could afford the switch?"

This almost caught Steven off guard. For an instant he panicked. He glanced at Josef, who was pouring a drink behind the bar. He had apparently been listening, and for an instant he looked back at Steven with an all-knowing smirk. Steven felt the full confidence Josef had in his abilities as the one who always spoke for him whenever Josef struggled to formulate a sentence.

Steven set down a plate of preservative-rich roast beef with a portion of previously bagged salad in front of the inquisition.

"Oh, God," he said as the plate left his hand and the cup of premixed ice tea was set down. "Absolutely anything would be better than Cigarette's. How about Quitter's?"

The health inspector laughed and began to tuck into his roast beef.

"Anything else for now?" asked Steven dutifully.

"No, thank you, Steven; everything's perfect," replied the inspector.

"Enjoy," Steven concluded with a smile.

He walked back into the kitchen to get a few bowls of intense-smelling soup for some regulars who sat well away from the health inspector. Steven knew that the soup tasted of unnecessarily forbidden, fulfilling, and heartwarming natural pleasure. Before grabbing the bowls to place them on the serving tray, he grabbed Josef's ass hard with both hands, startling him and causing his body to firm up for an instant. Steven whispered in Josef's ear, close enough that Josef could feel the warmth of Steven's breath directly in his mind.

"Nothing could ever be better than Cigarette's," he said, with an aggressiveness mixed with anger and sensuality. "Nothing."

Then he returned to work.

Chapter 26, Cerberus Forgives

To have your prize right in front of you, confidently secured in anticipation of your whims, is the finality of any reasonable animal's instinctual motives—to possess what you want, to enjoy it as you please. For an animal, the prize is unquestioned and a product of need or instinct. What the prize is for a human being, though, once their basic needs have been satisfied, can only be discovered through a lifetime of personal exploration. Each achievement of a goal will only be satisfactory for a short period of time thereafter. Each person will always be hungry for something: food, love, the absence of pain, power, pleasure, rest, expression, meaning, freedom, acknowledgement. This "something" changes constantly. But the most pressing hunger is the hunger itself. The most basic desire is to keep oneself alive and able to continue desiring.

Eating and enjoyment are nearly synonymous for most creatures, especially when their hunger is extreme. Only then can they know the true pleasure of consumption. Humans have certainly synthesized this type of food-lust better than any competing animals. The desire to savor, the desire to *experience* food, is a powerful force reserved for the elite. Even the desire to reminisce about and share their previous eating experiences, as if they were the most worthy of achievements, is necessary to complete the whole experience.

Most people will never know this kind of power over their prize. They take their scraps and fill up on them satisfactorily out of necessity only. They will enjoy the sloppy consumption but never have the capacity to savor and appreciate the true flavor and blessing of the fruits of their conquest. And once the experience is over? It is forgotten and perhaps never really understood at all. The dog snarls when the hand that feeds him attempts to remove his dish prior to him finishing the meal, because he has been hungry before and he has a realistic uncertainty about the future. Then the food is gone. It was good, but what's next? The dog doesn't have the luxury of considering exactly what *it is,* or what *it means.* Perhaps that doesn't even matter, but why then should the larger, more evolved human brain be so involved with this kind of search after his basic needs are satisfied? Should we not just rest and wait? Or should we take as much as we can until we die?

The smell of the prize in front of the beast creates such a rush. Instances of anticipation exponentially increase the first wave of pleasure when the teeth pull the juices from the meal onto the tongue. Even this is only the beginning of an enjoyable voyage, but exactly *how great it is* remains a sensual mystery. Your anticipation builds as you cradle your impending conquest and assess your prize with your eyes. Then the journey. Then the pleasure of arrival. As soon you start ripping your desires off their respective bones, or away from their various attachments, you are already receiving messages of reward from your brain. Pleasure. Contentment. Such good fortune to be alive.

***

Cerberus felt the reward of being fed something delicious each time he wolfed it down. His hunger suggested that he could enjoy eating like this forever. But there was no pleasure delay or anticipatory enjoyment; it was a feeling of urgency that propelled him as he gulped down the ground, heavily marbled red-and-white meat in the bowl beneath him. It was soft and savory and slightly warm. His food was not warm because it was as fresh as his instincts led him to believe, but it was in fact just removed from the microwave in order to thaw out a somewhat frozen center. Even so, the warmth of the meat wads was so invigorating that it gave him energy even before his organs began to break down the calories.

Cerberus made his way through the bowls quickly, but each time his pace slowed as his belly filled with the heavy and slightly sour meal. The last bite was the least satisfying, but he still licked the bloody remnants from every corner. In fact, the last quarter of his bowl he somewhat forced down. The opportunity for another animal or even insects to enjoy any of his leftovers could not be chanced.

As a dog, it is not like Cerberus cared whatsoever, but he had put on a few extra pounds lately as a result of overflowing bowls of the tastiest meat he had ever enjoyed. He felt satisfied and sleepy as he lay down and drifted off to sleep with his slightly stretched belly full, victorious over his world. A victory over evolution. He was surviving. In fact he was thriving.

Consumption was the highest of the pleasure-producing instincts and was not interchangeable. Scraps just didn't seem like scraps to a dog. They were dominance. If only Cerberus could ever understand exactly how profound his own food-related dominance really was.

***

Steven opened up the back door to Cigarette's, and Cerberus rolled over on his matt to see his master. Steven watched as the dog shuffled up to his feet a little more awkwardly than usual, due to the size of his belly.

"Geez, Cerby, you really have been taking one for the team lately! You chubby little bugger." Steven smiled and motioned for Cerberus to come inside.

"Come on now," Steven said, happy to see Cerberus listening to him. "You're such a loyal member of the family. Good boy."

Any transition without pressure was favorable to Cerberus, whether it was in the door or out the door, off the leash and even sometimes back onto the security of the leash. A transition without pressure was stimulation and he loved being praised for following directions. Cerberus began eating without pause as soon as his dish was set down in front of him and Steven went to fetch him a fresh bowl of water. By the time he returned, Cerberus has licked

378

his bowl clean and was now licking the light reddish stains off his jowls. He wagged his tail.

"Well, we are almost out of your food, buddy, and then it will be back to the regular." Steven patted Cerberus's head and scratched under his chin as the dog leaned back, stretching in bliss. "It's probably for the best too, or you might end up snapping your front peg!"

Steven felt such a twister of emotions saying this. He felt a little bad for Cerberus for his trauma and also felt a little bad for running out of what seemed like Cerberus's favorite food. Then he felt a brief pang of fear. The potential for their discovery still loomed. The next feeling he had was the crushing urgency for the plan's completion. He brushed it off, and pushed the backdoor open with his hip, allowing Cerberus to pass by on his way outside. The leash's end was conveniently left on the stoop and Steven clipped in Cerberus's collar as he began to lap away at the water bowl, washing down his meal.

Steven looked up at the pinkish hue in the sky and shook his head, feeling content, albeit a bit uncomfortable for getting lost in the moment. He knew it was the city's pollution that amplified this colorful phenomenon. Maybe, just maybe, right now he was allowed not to care, though, and to enjoy the spectacle. When he lowered his head and scanned his immediate surroundings, things were less pleasant. The garbage and general roughness of the abandoned building across the vacant lot in front of him stank of failure and miscalculations.

He thought about the last few months and how stressful yet stimulating they had been. Perhaps the last true measure of equilibrium, the final fulcrum pivotal point below the lever of happiness, was in fact the midpoint between balance and imbalance itself. The derivative of exponential impossible perfection. He glanced across the empty street, hoping that no one had been watching him enjoy his private thoughts.

Cerberus hopped slowly in a few circles before settling down on his bed in the morning sun. He closed his eyes immediately as he awaited sleep. A slightly bad taste had formed

in Steven's mouth and he attributed this to the smell of the

remnants in the plastic dish he was holding. He always tried not to

touch the wet insides and hung the bowl by the rim with his index

finger. He scanned the horizon again. No one was there. Any

moment someone could come, though, and he felt that he had

tempted fate long enough.

He scraped his tongue with his top teeth, attempting to pool

the unwanted taste at the front of his mouth before spitting it out to

the side of the concrete step. Cerberus looked to be asleep.

"See you for dinner Cerberus." Steven said quietly to

himself as he turned his back on the outside world, swinging the

dog food dish back and forth on his finger as the door slammed

closed behind him.

The End

Cerberus & Cigarette's

Artwork courtesy of www.jdwarpaint.com

Acknowledgments

Thank you to my incredible partner Athena Zandboer for your love throughout the highs and lows of this project and for encouraging me to stay true to my vision.

Thank you to my editor David Antrobus for challenging me to grow as a writer.

Thank you to my parents Ron and Audrey who gave me the foundation to explore.

Thank you to my friends and family who have supported me so much.